Miss Ludington's Sister

Edward Bellamy

Contents

MISS LUDINGTON'S SISTER

BY

Edward Bellamy

CHAPTER I.

The happiness of some lives is distributed pretty evenly over the whole stretch from the cradle to the grave, while that of others comes all at once, glorifying some particular epoch and leaving the rest in shadow. During one, five, or ten blithe years, as the case may be, all the springs of life send up sweet waters; joy is in the very air we breathe; happiness seems our native element. During this period we know what is the zest of living, as compared with the mere endurance of existence, which is, perhaps, the most we have attained to before or since. With men this culminating epoch comes often in manhood, or even at maturity, especially with men of arduous and successful careers. But with women it comes most frequently perhaps in girlhood and young womanhood. Particularly is this wont to be the fact with women who do not marry, and with whom, as the years glide on, life becomes lonelier and its interests fewer.

By the time Miss Ida Ludington was twenty-five years old she recognised that she had done with happiness, and that the pale pleasures of memory were all which remained to her.

It was not so much the mere fact that her youth was past, saddening though that might be, which had so embittered her life, but the peculiarly cruel manner in which it had been taken from her.

The Ludingtons were one of the old families of Hilton, a little farming village among the hills of Massachusetts. They were not rich, but were well-to-do, lived in the largest house in the place, and were regarded somewhat as local magnates. Miss Ludington's childhood had been an exceptionally happy one, and as a girl she had been the belle of the village. Her beauty, together, with her social position and amiability of disposition, made her the idol of the young men, recognised leader of the girls, and the animating and central figure in the social life of the place.

She was about twenty years old, at the height of her beauty and in the full tide of youthful enjoyment, when she fell ill of a dreadful disease, and for a long time lay between life and death. Or, to state the case more accurately, the girl did die--it was a sad and faded woman who rose from that bed of sickness.

The ravages of disease had not left a vestige of her beauty--it was hopelessly gone. The luxuriant, shining hair had fallen out and been replaced by a scanty growth of washed-out hue; the lips, but yesterday so full, and red, and tempting, were thin, and drawn, and colourless, and the rose-leaf complexion had given place to an aspect so cruelly pitted, seamed, and scarred that even friends did not recognize her.

The fading of youth is always a melancholy experience with women; but in most cases the process is so gradual as to temper the poignancy of regret, and perhaps often to prevent its being experienced at all except as a vague sentiment.

But in Miss Ludington's case the transition had been piteously sharp and abrupt.

With others, ere youth is fully past its charms are well-nigh forgotten in the engrossments of later years; but with her there had been nothing to temper the bitterness of her loss.

During the long period of invalidism which followed her sickness her only solace was a miniature of herself, at the age of seventeen, painted on ivory, the daguerrotype process not having come into use at this time, which was toward the close of the third decade of the present century.

Over this picture she brooded hours together when no one was near, studying the bonny, gladsome face through blinding tears, and sometimes murmuring incoherent words of tenderness.

Her young friends occasionally came to sit with her, by way of enlivening the weary hours of an invalid's day. At such times she would listen with patient indifference while they sought to interest her with current local gossip, and as soon as possible would turn the conversation back to the old happy days before her sickness. On this topic she was never weary of talking, but it was impossible to induce her to take any interest in the present.

She had caused a locket to be made, to contain the ivory miniature of herself as a girl, and always wore it on her bosom.

In no way could her visitors give her more pleasure than by asking to see this picture, and expressing their admiration of it. Then her poor, disfigured face would look actually happy, and she would exclaim, "Was she not beautiful?" "I do not think it flattered her, do you?" and with other similar expressions indicate her sympathy with the admiration expressed. The absence of anything like self-consciousness in the delight she took in these tributes to the charms of her girlish self was pathetic in its completeness. It was indeed not as herself, but as another, that she thought of this fair girl, who had vanished from the earth, leaving a picture as her sole memento. How, indeed, could it be otherwise when she looked from the picture to the looking-glass, and contrasted the images? She mourned for her girlish self, which had been so cruelly effaced from the world of life, as for a person, near and precious to her beyond the power of words to express, who had died.

From the time that she had first risen from the sick-bed, where she had suffered so sad a transformation, nothing could induce her to put on the brightly coloured gowns, beribboned, and ruffled, and gaily trimmed, which she had worn as a girl; and as soon as she was able she carefully folded and put them away in lavender, like relics of the dead. For herself, she dressed henceforth in drab or black.

For three or four years she remained more or less an invalid. At the end of that time she regained a fair measure of health, although she seemed not likely ever to be strong.

In the meanwhile her school-mates and friends had pretty much all married, or been given in marriage. She was a stranger to the new set of young people which had come on the stage since her day, while her former companions lived in a world of new interests, with which she had nothing in common. Society, in reorganizing itself, had left her on the outside. The present had moved on, leaving her behind with the past. She asked nothing better. If she was nothing to the present, the present was still less to her. As to society, her sensitiveness to the unpleasant impression made by her personal appearance rendered social gatherings distasteful to her, and she wore a heavy veil when she went to church.

She was an only child. Her mother had long been dead, and when about this time her father died she was left without near kin. With no ties of contemporary interest to hold her to the present she fell more and more under the influence of the habit of retrospection.

The only brightness of colour which life could ever have for her lay behind in the girlhood which had ended but yesterday, and was yet so completely ended. She found her only happiness in the recollections of that period which she retained. These were the only goods she prized, and it was the grief of her life that, while she had strong boxes for her money, and locks and keys for her silver and her linen, there was no device whereby she could protect her store of memories from the slow wasting of forgetfulness.

She lived with a servant quite alone in the old Ludington homestead, which it was her absorbing care to keep in precisely the same condition, even to the arrangement of the furniture, in which it had always been.

If she could have insured the same permanence in the village of Hilton, outside the homestead enclosure, she would have been spared the cause of her keenest unhappiness. For the hand of change was making havoc with the village: the railroad had come, shops had been built, and stores and new houses were going up on every side, and the beautiful hamlet, with its score or two of old-fashioned dwellings, which had been the scene of her girlhood, was in a fair way to be transformed into a vile manufacturing village.

Miss Ludington, to whom every stick and stone of the place was dear, could not walk abroad without missing some ancient landmark removed since she had passed that way before, perhaps a tree felled, some meadow, that had been a playground of her childhood, dug up for building-lots, or a row of brick tenements going up on the site of a sacred grove.

Her neighbours generally had succumbed to the rage for improvement, as they called it. There was a general remodelling and modernizing of houses, and, where nothing more expensive could be afforded, the paint-brush wrought its cheap metamorphosis. "You wouldn't know Hilton was the same place," was the complacent verdict of her neighbours, to which Miss Ludington sorrowfully assented.

It would be hard to describe her impotent wrath, her sense of outrage and irreparable loss, as one by one these changes effaced some souvenir of her early life. The past was once dead already; they were killing it a second time. Her feelings at length became so intolerable that she kept her house, pretty much ceasing to walk abroad.

At this period, when she was between thirty and thirty-five years old, a distant relative left her a large fortune. She had been well-to-do before, but now she was very rich. As her expenses had never exceeded a few hundred dollars a year, which had procured her everything she needed, it would be hard to imagine a person with less apparent use for a great deal of money. And yet no young rake, in the heyday of youth and the riot of hot blood, could have been more overjoyed at the falling to him of a fortune than was this sad-faced old maid. She became smiling and animated. She no longer kept at home, but walked abroad. Her step was quick and strong; she looked on at the tree-choppers, the builders, and the painters, at their nefarious work, no more in helpless grief and indignation, but with an unmistakable expression of triumph.

Presently surveyors appeared in the village, taking exact and careful measurements of the single broad and grassy street which formed the older part of it. Miss Ludington was closeted with a builder, and engrossed with estimates. The next year she left Hilton to the mercy of the vandals, and never returned.

But it was to another Hilton that she went.

The fortune she had inherited had enabled her to carry out a design which had been a day-dream with her ever since the transformation of the village had begun. Among the pieces of property left her was a large farm on Long Island several miles out of the city of Brooklyn. Here she had rebuilt the Hilton of her girlhood, in facsimile, with every change restored, every landmark replaced. In the midst of this silent village she had built for her residence an exact duplicate of the Ludington homestead, situated in respect to the rest of the village precisely as the original was situated in the real Hilton.

The astonishment of the surveyors and builders at the character of the work required of them was probably great, and their bills certainly were, though Miss Ludington would not have grudged the money had they been ten times greater. However, seeing that the part of the village duplicated consisted of but one broad maple-planted street, with not over thirty houses, mostly a story and a half, and that none of the buildings, except the school-house, the little meeting-house, and the homestead, were finished inside, the outlay was not greater than an elaborate plan of landscape gardening would have involved.

The furniture and fittings of the Massachusetts homestead, to the least detail, had been used to fit up its Long Island duplicate, and when all was complete and

Miss Ludington had settled down to housekeeping, she felt more at home than in ten years past.

True, the village which she had restored was empty; but it was not more empty than the other Hilton had been to her these many years, since her old schoolmates had been metamorphosed into staid fathers and mothers. These respectable persons were not the schoolmates and friends of her girlhood, and with no hard feelings toward them, she had still rather resented seeing them about, as tending to blur her recollections of their former selves, in whom alone she was interested.

That her new Long Island neighbours considered her mildly insane was to her the least of all concerns. The only neighbours she cared about were the shadowy forms which peopled the village she had rescued from oblivion, whose faces she fancied smiling gratefully at her from the windows of the homes she had restored to them.

For she had a notion that the spirits of her old neighbours, long dead, had found out this resurrected Hilton, and were grateful for the opportunity to revisit the unaltered scenes of their passion. If she had grieved over the removal of the old landmarks and the change in the appearance of the village, how much more hopelessly must they have grieved if indeed the dead revisit earth! The living, if their homes are broken up, can make them new ones, which, after a fashion, will serve the purpose; but the dead cannot. They are thenceforth homeless and desolate.

No sense of having benefited living persons would have afforded Miss Ludington the pleasure she took in feeling that, by rebuilding ancient Hilton, she had restored homes to these homeless ones.

But of all this fabric of the past which she had resurrected, the central figure was the school-girl Ida Ludington. The restored village was the mausoleum of her youth.

Over the great old-fashioned fireplace, in the sitting-room of the homestead which she had rebuilt in the midst of the village, she had hung a portrait in oil, by the first portrait-painter then in the country. It was an enlarged copy of the little likeness on ivory which had formerly been so great a solace to her.

The portrait was executed with extremely life-like effect, and was fondly believed by Miss Ludington to be a more accurate likeness in some particulars than the ivory picture itself.

It represented a very beautiful girl of seventeen or eighteen, although already possessing the ripened charms of a woman. She was dressed in white, with a low bodice, her luxuriant golden hair, of a rare sheen and fineness, falling upon beautifully moulded shoulders. The complexion was of a purity that needed the faint tinge of pink in the cheeks to relieve it of a suspicion of pallor. The eyes were of the deepest, tenderest violet, full of the light of youth, and the lips were smiling.

It was, indeed, no wonder that Miss Ludington had mourned the vanishing from earth of this delectable maiden with exceeding bitterness, or that her heart yet yearned after her with an aching tenderness across the gulf of years.

How bright, how vivid, how glowing had been the life of that beautiful girl! How real as compared with her own faint and faded personality, which, indeed, had shone these many years only by the light reflected from that young face! And yet that life, in its strength and brightness, had vanished like an exhalation, and its elements might no more be recombined than the hues of yesterday's dawn.

Miss Ludington had hung the portraits of her father and mother with immortelles, but the frame of the girl's picture she had wound with deepest crape.

Her father and mother she did not mourn as one without hope, believing that she should see them some day in another world; but from the death of change which the girl had died no Messiah had ever promised any resurrection.

CHAPTER II.

The solitude in which Miss Ludington lived had become, through habit, so endeared to her that when, a few years after she had been settled in her ghostly village, a cousin died in poverty, bequeathing to her with his last breath a motherless infant boy, it was with great reluctance that she accepted the charge. She would have willingly assumed the support of the child, but if it had been possible would have greatly preferred providing for him elsewhere to bringing him home with her. This, however, was impracticable, and so there came to be a baby in the old maid's house.

Little Paul De Riemer was two years old when he was brought to live with Miss Ludington--a beautiful child, with loving ways, and deep, dark, thoughtful eyes. When he was first taken into the sitting-room, the picture of the smiling girl over the fireplace instantly attracted his gaze, and, putting out his arms, he cooed to it. This completed the conquest of Miss Ludington, whose womanly heart had gone out to the winsome child at first sight.

As the boy grew older his first rational questions were about the pretty lady in the picture, and, he was never so happy as when Miss Ludington took him upon her knee and told him stories about her for hours together.

These stories she always related in the third person, for it would only puzzle and grieve the child to intimate to him that there was anything in common between the radiant girl he had been taught to call Ida and the withered woman whom he called Aunty. What, indeed, had they in common but their name? and it had been so long since any one had called her Ida, that Miss Ludington scarcely felt that the name belonged to her present self at all.

In their daily walks about the village she would tell the little boy endless stories about incidents which had befallen Ida at this spot or that. She was never weary of telling, or he of listening to, these tales, and it was wonderful how the artless sympathy of the child comforted the lone woman.

One day, when he was eight years old, finding himself alone in the sitting-room, the lad, after contemplating Ida's picture for a long time, piled one chair on another, and climbing upon the structure, put up his chubby lips to the painted lips of the portrait and kissed them with right good-will. Just then Miss Ludington came in, and saw what he was doing. Seizing him in her arms, she cried over him and kissed him till he was thoroughly frightened.

A year or two later, on his announcing one day his intention to marry Ida when he grew up, Miss Ludington explained to him that she was dead. He was quite overcome with grief at this intelligence, and for a long time refused to be comforted.

And so it was, that never straying beyond the confines of the eerie village, and having no companion but Miss Ludington, the boy fell scarcely less than she under the influence of the beautiful girl who was the presiding genius of the place.

As he grew older, far from losing its charm, Ida's picture laid upon him a new spell. Her violet eyes lighted his first love-dreams. She became his ideal of feminine loveliness, drawing to herself, as the sun draws mist, all the sentiment and dawning passion of the youth. In a word, he fell in love with her.

Of course he knew now who she had been. Long before as soon as he was old enough to understand it, this had been explained to him. But though he was well aware that neither on earth nor in heaven, nor anywhere in the universe, did she any more exist, that knowledge was quite without effect upon the devotion which she had inspired. The matter indeed, presented itself in a very simple way to his mind. "If I had never seen her picture," he said one day to Miss Ludington, "I should never have known that my love was dead, and I should have gone seeking her through all the world, and wondering what was the reason I could not find her."

Miss Ludington was over sixty years of age and Paul was twenty-two when he finished his course at college. She had naturally supposed that, on going out into the world, mixing with young men and meeting young women, he would outgrow his romantic fancy concerning Ida; but the event was very different. As year after year he returned home to spend his vacations, it was evident that his visionary passion was strengthening rather than losing its hold upon him.

But the strangest thing of all was the very peculiar manner in which, during the last vacation preceding his graduation, he began to allude to Ida in his conversations with Miss Ludington. It was, indeed, so peculiar that when, after his return to college, she recalled the impression left upon her mind, she was constrained to think that she had, somehow, totally misunderstood him; for he had certainly seemed to talk as if Ida, instead of being that most utterly, pathetically dead of all dead things--the past self of a living person--were possibly not dead at all: as if, in fact she might have a spiritual existence, like that ascribed to the souls of those other dead whose bodies are laid in the grave.

Decidedly, she must have misunderstood him.

Some months later, on one of the last days of June, he graduated. Miss Ludington would have attended the graduation exercises but for the fact that her long seclusion from society made the idea of going away from home and mingling with strangers intolerable. She had expected him home the morning after his graduation. When, however, she came downstairs, expecting to greet him at the breakfast-table, she found instead a letter from him, which, to her further astonishment, consisted of several closely written sheets. What could have possessed him to write her this laborious letter on the very day of his return?

The letter began by telling her that he had accepted an invitation from a classmate, and should not be home for a couple of days. "But this is only an excuse," he went on; "the true reason that I do not at once return is that you may have a day or two to think over the contents of this letter before you see me; for what I have to say will seem very startling to you at first. I was trying to prepare you for it when I talked, as you evidently thought, so strangely, about Ida, the last time I was at home; but you were only mystified, and I was not ready to explain. A certain timidity held me back. It was so great a matter that I was afraid to broach it by word of mouth lest I might fail to put it in just the best way before your mind, and its strangeness might terrify you before you could be led to consider its reasonableness. But, now that I am coming home to stay, I should not be able to keep it from you, and it has seemed to me better to write you in this way, so that you may have time fully to debate the matter with your own heart before you see me. Do you remember the last evening that I was at home, my asking you if you did not sometimes have a sense of Ida's presence? You looked at me as if you thought I were losing my wits. What did I mean, you asked, by speaking of her as a living person? But I was not ready to speak, and I put you off.

"I am going to answer your question now. I am going to tell you how and why I believe that she is neither lost nor dead, but a living and immortal spirit. For this, nothing less than this, is my absolute assurance, the conviction which I ask you to share.

"But stop, let us go back. Let us assume nothing. Let us reason it all out carefully from the beginning. Let me forget that I am her lover. Let me be stiff; and slow, and formal as a logician, while I prove that my darling lives for ever. And you, follow me carefully, to see if I slip. Forget what ineffable thing she is to you; forget what it is to you that she lives. Do not let your eyes fill; do not let your brain swim. It would be madness to believe it if it is not true. Listen, then:-- You know that men speak of human beings, taken singly, as individuals. It is taken for granted in the common speech that the individual is the unit of humanity, not to be subdivided. That is, indeed, what the etymology of the word means. Nevertheless, the slightest reflection will cause any one to see that this assumption is a most mistaken one. The individual is no more the unit of humanity than is the tribe or family; but, like them, is a collective noun, and stands for a number of distinct persons, related one to another in a particular way, and having certain features of resemblance. The persons composing a family are related both collaterally and by succession or descent, while the persons composing an individual are related by succession only. They are called infancy, childhood, youth, manhood, maturity, age, and dotage.

"These persons are very unlike one another. Striking physical, mental, and moral differences exist between them. Infancy and childhood are incomprehensible to manhood, and manhood not less so to them. The youth looks forward with disgust to the old age which is to follow him, and the old man has far more in common with other old men, his own contemporaries, than with the youth who preceded him. How frequently do we see the youth vicious and depraved, and the man who follows him upright and virtuous, hating iniquity! How often, on the other hand, is a pure and innocent girlhood succeeded by a dissolute and shameless womanhood! In many cases age looks back upon youth with inexpressible longing and tenderness, and quite as often with shame and remorse; but in all cases with the same consciousness of profound contrast, and of a great gulf fixed between.

"If the series of persons which constitutes an individual could by any magic be brought together and these persons confronted with one another, in how many cases would the result be mutual misunderstanding, disgust, and even animosity? Suppose, for instance, that Saul, the persecutor of the disciples of Jesus, who held the garments of them that stoned Stephen, should be confronted with his later self, Paul the apostle, would there not be reason to anticipate a stormy interview? For there is no more ground to suppose that Saul would be converted to Paul's view than the reverse. Each was fully persuaded in his own mind as to what he did.

"But for the fact that each one of the persons who together constitute an individual is well off the field before his successor comes upon it, we should not infrequently see the man collaring his own youth, handing him over to the authorities, and prefering charges against him as a rascally fellow.

"Not by any means are the successive persons of an individual always thus out of harmony with one another. In many, perhaps in a majority, of cases, the same general principles and ideals are recognized by the man which were adopted by the boy, and as much sympathy exists between them as is possible in view of the different aspects which the world necessarily presents to youth and age. In such cases, no doubt, could the series of persons constituting the individual be brought together, a scene of inexpressibly tender and intimate communion would ensue.

"But, though no magic may bring back our past selves to earth, may we not hope to meet them hereafter in some other world? Nay, must we not expect so to meet them if we believe in the immortality of human souls? For if our past selves, who were dead before we were alive, had no souls, then why suppose our present selves have any? Childhood, youth, and manhood are the sweetest, the fairest, the noblest, the strongest of the persons who together constitute an individual. Are they soulless? Do they go down in darkness to oblivion while immortality is reserved for the withered soul of age? If we must believe that there is but one soul to all the persons of an individual it would be easier to believe that it belongs to youth or manhood, and that age is soulless. For if youth, strong-winged and ardent, full of fire and power, perish, leaving nothing behind save a few traces in the memory, how shall the flickering spirit of age have strength to survive the blast of death?

"The individual, in its career of seventy years, has not one body, but many, each wholly new. It is a commonplace of physiology that there is not a particle in the body to-day that was in it a few years ago. Shall we say that none of these bodies has a soul except the last, merely because the last decays more suddenly than the others?

"Or is it maintained that, although there is such utter diversity-- physical, mental, moral--between infancy and manhood, youth and age, nevertheless, there is a certain essence common to them all, and persisting unchanged through them all, and that this is the soul of the individual? But such an essence as should be the same in the babe and the man, the youth and the dotard, could be nothing more than a colourless abstraction, without distinctive qualities of any kind--a mere principle of life like the fabled jelly protoplasm. Such a fancy reduces the hope of immortality to an absurdity.

"No! no! It is not any such grotesque or fragmentary immortality that God has given us. The Creator does not administer the universe on so niggardly a plan. Either there is no immortality for us which is intelligible or satisfying, or childhood, youth, manhood, age, and all the other persons who make up an individual, live for ever, and one day will meet and be together in God's eternal present; and when the several souls of an individual are in harmony no doubt He will perfect their felicity by joining them with a tie that shall be incomparably more tender and intimate than any earthly union ever dreamed of, constituting a life one yet manifold--a harp of many strings, not struck successively as here on earth, but blending in rich accord.

"And now I beg you not to suppose that what I have tried to demonstrate is any hasty or ill-considered fancy. It was, indeed, at first but a dream with which the eyes of my sweet mistress inspired me, but from a dream it has grown into a belief, and in these last months into a conviction which I am sure nothing can shake. If you can share it the long mourning of your life will be at an end. For my own part I could never return to the old way of thinking without relapsing into unutterable despair. To do so would be virtually to give up faith in any immortality at all worth speaking of. For it is the long procession of our past selves, each with its own peculiar charm and incommunicable quality, slipping away from us as we pass on, and not the last self of all whom the grave entraps, which constitutes our chief contribution to mortality. What shall it avail for the grave to give up its handful if there be no immortality for this great multitude? God would not mock us thus. He has power not only over the grave, but over the viewless sepulchre of the past, and not one of the souls to which he has ever given life will be found wanting on the day when he makes up his jewels."

CHAPTER III.

To understand the impression which Paul's letter produced upon Miss Ludington imagine, in the days before the resurrection of the dead was preached, with what effect the convincing announcement of that doctrine would have fallen on the ears of one who had devoted her life to hopeless regrets over the ashes of a friend.

And yet at no time have men been wholly without belief in some form of survival beyond the grave, and such a bereaved woman of antiquity would merely have received a more clear and positive assurance of what she had vaguely imagined before. But that there was any resurrection for her former self--that the bright youth which she had so yearned after and lamented could anywhere still exist, in a mode however shadowy, Miss Ludington had never so much as dreamed.

There might be immortality for all things else; the birds and beasts, and even the lowest forms of life, might, under some form, in some world, live again; but no priest had ever promised, nor any poet ever dreamed, that the title of a man's past selves to a life immortal is as indefeasible as that of his present self.

It did not occur to her to doubt, to quibble, or to question, concerning the grounds of this great hope. From the first moment that she comprehended the purport of Paul's argument, she had accepted its conclusion as an indubitable revelation, and only wondered that she had never thought of it herself, so natural, so inevitable, so incontrovertible did it seem.

And as a sunburst in an instant transforms the sad fields of November into a bright and cheerful landscape, so did this revelation suddenly illumine her sombre life.

All day she went about the house and the village like one in a dream, smiling and weeping, and reading Paul's letter over and over, through eyes swimming with a joy unutterable.

In the afternoon, with tender, tremulous fingers, she removed the crape from the frame of Ida's picture, which it had draped for so many years. As she was performing this symbolic act, it seemed to the old lady that the fair young face smiled upon her. "Forgive me!" she murmured. "How could I have ever thought you dead!"

It was not till evening that her servants reminded her that she had not eaten that day, and induced her to take food.

The next afternoon Paul arrived. He had not been without very serious doubt as to the manner in which his argument for the immortality of past selves might impress Miss Ludington. A mild melancholy such as hers sometimes becomes sweet by long indulgence. She might not welcome opinions which revolutionized the fixed ideas of her life, even though they should promise a more cheerful philosophy. If she did not accept his belief, but found it chimerical and visionary, the effect of its announcement upon her mind could only be unpleasantly disturbing. It was, therefore, not without some anxiety that he approached the house.

But his first glimpse of her, as she stood in the door awaiting him, dissipated his apprehensions. She wore a smiling face, and the deep black in which she always dressed was set off, for the first time since his knowledge of her, with a bit or two of bright colour.

She said not a word, but, taking him by the hand, led him into the sitting-room.

That morning she had sent into Brooklyn for immortelles, and had spent the day in festooning them about Ida's picture, so that now the sweet girlish face seemed smiling upon them out of a veritable bower of the white flowers of immortality.

In the days that followed, Miss Ludington seemed a changed woman, such blitheness did the new faith she had found bring into her life. The conviction that the past was deathless, and her bright girlhood immortal, took all the melancholy out of retrospection. Nay, more than that, it turned retrospection into anticipation. She no longer viewed her youth-time through the pensive haze of memory, but the rosy mist of hope. She should see it again, for was it not safe with God? Her pains to guard the memory of the beautiful past, to preserve it from the second death of forgetfulness, were now all needless; she could trust it with God, to be restored to her in his eternal present, its lustre undimmed, and no trait missing.

The laying aside of her mourning garb was but one indication of the change that had come over her.

The whole household, from scullion to coachman, caught the inspiration of her brighter mood. The servants laughed aloud about the house. The children of the gardener, ever before banished to other parts of the grounds, played unrebuked in the sacred street of the silent village.

As for Paul, since the revelation had come to him that the lady of his love was no mere dream of a life for ever vanished, but was herself alive for evermore, and that he should one day meet her, his love had assumed a colour and a reality it had never possessed before. To him this meant all it would have meant to the lover of a material maiden, to be admitted to her immediate society.

The sense of her presence in the village imparted to the very air a fine quality of intoxication. The place was her shrine, and he lived in it as in a sanctuary.

It was not as if he should have to wait many years, till death, before he should see her. As soon as he gave place to the later self which was to succeed him, he should be with her. Already his boyish self had no doubt greeted her, and she had taken in her arms the baby Paul who had held his little arms out to her picture twenty years before.

To be in love with the spirit of a girl, however beautiful she might have been when on earth, would doubtless seem to most young men a very chimerical sort of passion; but Paul, on the other hand, looked upon the species of attraction which they called love as scarcely more than a gross appetite. During his absence from home he had seen no woman's face that for a moment rivalled Ida's portrait. Shy and fastidious, he had found no pleasure in ladies' society, and had listened to his classmates' talk of flirtations and conquests with secret contempt. What did they know of love? What had their coarse and sensuous ideas in common with the rare and delicate passion to which his heart was dedicated--a love asking and hoping for no reward, but sufficient to itself?

He had spent but a few weeks at home when Miss Ludington began to talk quite seriously to him about studying for some profession. He was rather surprised at this, for he had supposed she would be glad to have him at home, for a while at lease, now that he had done with college. To Paul, at this time, the idea of any pursuit which would take him away from the village was extremely distasteful, and he had no difficulty in finding excuses enough for procrastinating a step for which, indeed, no sort of urgency could be pretended.

He was to be Miss Ludington's heir, and any profession which he might adopt would be purely ornamental at most.

Finding that he showed no disposition to consider a profession she dropped that point and proposed that he should take six months of foreign travel, as a sort of rounding off of his college course. To the advantages of this project he was, however, equally insensible. When she urged it on him, he said, "Why, aunty, one would say you were anxious to get rid of me. Don't we get on well together? Have you taken a dislike to me? I'm sure I'm very comfortable here. I don't want to do anything different, or to go off anywhere. Why won't you let me stay with you?"

And so she had to let the matter drop.

The truth was she had become anxious to get him away; but it was on his account, not hers.

In putting his room to rights one day since his return from college she had come upon a scrap of paper containing some verses addressed "To Ida." Paul had rather a pretty knack at turning rhymes, and the tears came to Miss Ludington's eyes as she read these lines. They were an attempt at a love sonnet, throbbing with passion, and yet so mystical in some of the allusions that nothing but her knowledge of Paul's devotion to Ida would have given her a clue to his meaning. She was filled with apprehension as she considered the effect which this infatuation, if it should continue to gain strength, might have upon one of Paul's dreamy temperament and excessive ideality. That she had devoted her own lonely and useless life to the cult of the past did not greatly matter, although in the light of her present happier faith she saw and regretted her mistake; but as for permitting Paul's life to be overshadowed by the same influence she could not consent to it. Something must be done to get him away from home, or at least to divert the current of his thought. The failure of her efforts to induce him to consider any scheme that involved his leaving the village threw her into a state of great uneasiness.

CHAPTER IV.

At about this time it chanced that Miss Ludington drove into Brooklyn one morning to do some shopping. She was standing at a counter in a large store, examining goods, when she became aware that a lady standing at another counter was attentively regarding her. The lady in question was of about her own height and age, her hair being nearly white, like Miss Ludington's; but it was evident from the hard lines of her face and her almost shabby dress that life had by no means gone so easily with her as with the lady she was regarding so curiously.

As Miss Ludington looked up she smiled, and, crossing the store, held out her hand. "Ida Ludington! don't you know me?" Miss Ludington scanned her face a moment, and then, clasping her outstretched hand, exclaimed, delightedly, "Why, Sarah Cobb, where did you come from?" and for the next quarter of an hour the two ladies, quite oblivious of the clerks who were waiting on them, and the customers who were jostling them, stood absorbed in the most animated conversation. They had been school-girls together in Hilton forty-five years before, and, not having met since Miss Ludington's removal from the village, had naturally a great deal to say.

"It is thirty years since I have seen any one from Hilton," said Miss Ludington at last, "and I'm not going to let you escape me. You must come out with me to my house and stay overnight, and we will talk old times over. I would not have missed you for anything."

Sarah Cobb, who had said that her name was now Mrs. Slater, and that she lived in New York, having removed there from Hilton only a few years previous, seemed nothing loth to accept her friend's invitation, and it was arranged that Miss Ludington should send her carriage to meet her at one of the Brooklyn ferries the

day following. Miss Ludington wanted to send the carriage to Mrs. Slater's residence in New York, but the latter said that it would be quite as convenient for her
to take it at the ferry.

After repeated injunctions not to fail of her appointment, Miss Ludington finally bade her old school-mate good-by and drove home in a state of pleased expectancy.

She entertained Paul at the tea-table with an account of her adventure, and
gave him an animated history of the Cobb family in general and Sarah in particular.
She had known Sarah ever since they both could walk, and during the latter part of
their school life they had been inseparable. The scholars had even christened them
"The Twins," because they were so much together and looked so much alike. Their
secrets were always joint property.

The next afternoon Miss Ludington went herself in the carriage to fetch her
friend from the ferry. She wanted to be with her and enjoy her surprise when she
first saw the restored Hilton on entering the grounds. In this respect her anticipa-
tions were fully justified.

The arrangement of the grounds was such that a high board fence protected the
interior from inquisitive passers-by on the highway, and the gate was set in a corner, so that no considerable part of the enclosure was visible from it. The gravelled
driveway, immediately after entering the grounds, took a sharp turn round the
corner of the gardener's cottage, which answered for a gatekeeper's lodge. The moment, however, it was out of sight from the highway it became transformed into a
country road, with wide, grassy borders and footpaths close to the rail fences, while
just ahead lay the silent village, with the small, brown, one-storey, one-roomed
school-house on one side of the green, and the little white box of a meeting-house,
with its gilt weathercock, on the other.

As this scene burst upon Mrs. Slater's view, her bewilderment was amusing
to witness. Her appearance for a moment was really as if she believed herself the
victim of some sort of magic, and suspected her friend of being a sorceress. Reas-
sured on this point by Miss Ludington's smiling explanation, her astonishment gave
place to the liveliest interest and curiosity. The carriage was forthwith stopped and
sent around to the stables, while the two friends went on foot through the village.
Every house, every fence-corner, every lilac-bush or clump of hollyhocks, or row of

currant-bushes in the gardens, suggested some reminiscence, and the two old ladies were presently laughing and crying at once. At every dwelling they lingered long, and went on reluctantly with many backward glances, and all their speech was but a repetition of, "Don't you remember this?" and "Do you remember that?"

Mrs Slater, having left Hilton but recently, was able to explain just what had been removed, replaced, or altered subsequent to Miss Ludington's flight. The general appearance of the old street, Mrs. Slater said, remained much the same, despite the changes which had driven Miss Ludington away; but new streets had been opened up, and the population of the village had trebled, and become largely foreign.

In their slow progress they came at last to the school-house.

The door was ajar, and they entered on tiptoe, like tardy scholars. With a glance of mutual intelligence they hung their hats, each on the one of the row of wooden pegs in the entry, which had been hers as a school-girl, and through the open door entered the silent school-room and sat down in the self-same seats in which two maidens, so unlike them, yet linked to them by so strangely tender a tie, had reigned as school-room belles nearly half a century before. In hushed voices, with moist eyes; and faces shining with the light of other days, those grey-haired women talked together of the scenes which that homely old room had witnessed, the long-silent laughter, and the voices, no more heard on earth, with which it had once echoed.

There in the corner stood a great wrought-iron stove, the counterpart of the one around whose red-hot sides they had shivered, in their short dresses, on cold winter mornings. On the walls hung the quaint maps of that period whence they had received geographical impressions, strangely antiquated now. Along one side of the room ran a black-board, on which they had been wont to demonstrate their ignorance of algebra and geometry to the complete satisfaction of the master, while behind them as they sat was a row of recitation benches, associated with so many a trying ordeal of school-girl existence.

"Do you ever think where the girls are in whose seats we are sitting?" said Mrs. Slater, musingly. "I can remember myself as a girl, more or less distinctly, and can even be sentimental about her; but it doesn't seem to me that I am the same person at all; I can't realize it."

"Of course you can't realize it. Why should you expect to realize what is not true?" replied Miss Ludington.

"But I am the same person," responded Mrs. Slater.

Miss Ludington regarded her with a smile.

"You have kept your looks remarkably, my dear," she said. "You did not lose them all at once, as I did; but isn't it a little audacious to try to pass yourself off as a school-girl of seventeen?"

Mrs. Slater laughed. "But I once was she, if I am not now," she said. "You won't deny that."

"I certainly shall deny it, with your permission," replied Ludington. "I remember her very well, and she was no more an old woman like you than you are a young girl like her."

Mrs. Slater laughed again. "How sharp you are getting, my dear!" she said. "Since you are so close after me, I shall have to admit that I have changed slightly in appearance in the forty odd years since we went to school at Hilton, and I'll admit that my heart is even less like a girl's than my face; but, though I have changed so much, I am still the same person, I suppose."

"Which do you mean?" inquired Miss Ludington. "You say in one breath that you are a changed person, and that you are the same person. If you are a changed person you can't be the same, and if you are the same you can't have changed."

"I should really like to know what you are driving at," said Mrs. Slater, calmly. "It seems to me that we are disputing about words."

"Oh, no, not about words! It is a great deal more than a question of words," exclaimed Miss Ludington. "You say that we old women and the girls who sat here forty years and more ago are the same persons, notwithstanding we are so completely transformed without and within. I say we are not the same, and thank God, for their sweet sakes, that we are not. Surely that is not a mere dispute about words."

"But, if we are not those girls, then what has become of them?" asked Mrs. Slater.

"You might better ask what had become of them if you had to seek them in us; but I will tell you what has become of them, Sarah. It is what will become of us when we, in our turn, vanish from earth, and the places that know us now shall know us no more. They are immortal with God, and we shall one day meet them over there."

"What a very odd idea!" exclaimed Mrs. Slater, regarding her friend with astonishment.

Miss Ludington flushed slightly as she replied, "I don't think it half so odd, and not nearly so repulsive, as your notion, that we old women are the mummies of the girls who came before us. It is easier, as well as far sweeter, for me to believe that our youth is somewhere immortal, than that it has been withered, shrivelled, desiccated into our old age. Oh, no, my dear, Paradise is not merely a garden of withered flowers! We shall find the rose and lily of our life blooming there."

The hours had slipped away unnoticed as the friends talked together, and now the lengthening shadows on the school-room floor recalled Miss Ludington to the present, and to the duties of a hostess.

As they walked slowly across the green toward the homestead, she told her friend more fully of this belief in the immortality of past selves which had so recently come to her, and especially how it had quite taken away the melancholy with which she had all her life before looked back upon her youth. Mrs. Slater listened in silence.

"Where on earth did you get that portrait?" she exclaimed, as Miss Ludington, after taking her on a tour through the house before tea, brought her into the sitting-room.

"Whom does it remind you of?" asked Miss Ludington.

"I know whom it reminds me of," replied Mrs. Slater; "but how it ever got here is what puzzles me."

"I thought you would recognize it," said Miss Ludington, with a pleased smile. "I suppose you think it odd you should never have seen it, considering whom it is of?"

"I do, certainly," replied Mrs. Slater.

"You see," explained Miss Ludington, "I did not have it painted till after I left Hilton. You remember that little ivory portrait of myself at seventeen, which I thought so much of after I lost my looks? Well, this portrait I had enlarged from that. I have always believed that it was very like, but you don't know what a reassurance it is to me to have you recognize it so instantly."

At the tea-table Paul appeared, and was introduced to Mrs. Slater, who regarded him with considerable interest. Miss Ludington had informed her that he was her cousin and heir, and had told her something of his romantic devotion to the Ida of the picture. Paul, who from Miss Ludington had learned all there was to be known about the persons and places of old Hilton, entered with much interest into the conversation of the ladies on the subject, and after tea accompanied them in their stroll through that part of the village which they had not inspected before.

When they returned to the house it was quite dark, and they had lights in the sitting-room, and refreshments were served. Mrs. Slater's eyes were frequently drawn toward the picture over the fireplace, and some reference of hers to the immortelles in which it was framed, turned the conversation upon the subject that Miss Ludington and she had been discussing in the school-house.

Mrs. Slater, whose conversation showed her to be a woman of no great culture, but unusual force of character and intelligence, expressed herself as interested in the idea of the immortality of past selves, but decidedly sceptical. Paul grew eloquent in maintaining its truth and reasonableness, and, indeed, that it was the only intelligible theory of immortality that was possible. The idea that the same soul successively animated infancy, childhood, youth, manhood, and maturity, was, he argued, but a modification of the curious East Indian dream of metempsychosis, according to which every soul is supposed to inhabit in turn innumerable bodies.

"You almost persuade me," said Mrs. Slater, at last. "But I never heard of the spirit of anybody's past self appearing to them. If there are such spirits, why have they never manifested themselves? Nobody every heard of the spirit of one's past self appearing at a spiritualist seance, for instance."

"There is one evidence among others," replied Paul. "that spiritualism is a fraud. The mediums merely follow the vulgar superstition in the kind of spirits that they claim to produce."

"Very likely you are right," said Mrs. Slater. "In fact, I presume you are quite right. And yet, if I really believed as you do, do you know what I would do? I would go to some of the spirit mediums over in New York, of whom the papers are giving such wonderful accounts, and let them try to materialize for me the spirit of my youth. Probably they couldn't do it, but possibly they might; and a mighty little sight, Mr. De Riemer, is more convincing than all the belief in the world. If I could see the spirit of my youth face to face, I should believe that it had a separate existence from my own. Otherwise, I don't believe I ever could."

"But the mediums are a set of humbugs!" exclaimed Paul; and then he added, "I beg your pardon. Perhaps you are a spiritualist?"

"You need not beg my pardon," said Mrs. Slater, good-humouredly. "I am not a spiritualist beyond thinking--and that is only lately--that there may possibly be something in it, after all. Perhaps there may be, for example, one part of truth to a hundred parts of fraud. I really don't believe there is more. Now, as you think the mediums humbugs, and I am sure most of them are, their failure to accomplish anything would not shake your faith in your theory, and you would only have lost an evening and the fee you paid the medium. On the other hand, there is a bare possibility--mind you, I think it is no more than that--a bare possibility, say the smallest possible chance, but a chance--that you would see--her," and Mrs. Slater glanced at the portrait.

Paul turned pale.

Miss Ludington, with much agitation, exclaimed, "If I thought there was any possibility of that, do you suppose, Sarah, that I would consider time or money?"

"I don't suppose you would," replied Mrs. Slater. "You would not need to; but the money is something which I should have to consider, if it were my case. The best materializing mediums charge pretty well. Mrs. Legrand, who I believe is con- sidered the leading light just now, charges fifty dollars for a private seance. Now, fifty dollars, I suppose, does not seem a large sum to you, but it would be a great deal for a poor woman like me to spend. And yet if I believed this wonderful thing that you believe, and I thought there was one chance in a million that this woman could demonstrate it to me by the assurance of sight, I would live on crusts from the gutter till I had earned the money to go to her."

Paul rose from his chair, and, after walking across the floor once or twice, stood leaning his arm on the mantelpiece. He cleared his throat, and said:

"Have you ever seen this Mrs. Legrand yourself? I mean, have you ever been present at one of her seances?"

"Not on my own account," replied Mrs. Slater. "It was a mere accident my chancing to know anything about her. I have a friend, a Mrs. Rhinehart, who has recently lost her husband, and she got in a way of going to this Mrs. Legrand's se- ances to see him, and once she took me with her."

Miss Ludington and Paul waited a moment, and then, perceiving that she was not going to say anything more, exclaimed in the same breath, "Did you see anything?"

"We saw the figure of a fine-looking man," replied Mrs. Slater. "We could distinguish his features and expression very plainly, and he seemed to recognize my friend. She said that it was her husband. Of course I know nothing about that. I had never seen him alive. It may all have been a humbug, as I was prepared to believe it; but I assure you it was a curious business, and I haven't got over the impression which it made on me, yet. I'm not given to believing in things that claim to be supernatural, but I will admit that what I saw that night was very strange. Humbug or no humbug, what she saw seemed to comfort my poor friend more than all the religions or philosophies ever revealed or invented could have done. You see, these are so vague, even when we try to believe them, and that was so plain."

A silence followed Mrs. Slater's words, during which she sat with an absent expression of countenance and a faraway look, as if recalling in fancy the scene which she had described. Miss Ludington's hands trembled as they lay together in her lap, and she was regarding the picture of the girl over the fireplace with a fixed and intense gaze, apparently oblivious of all else.

Paul broke the silence. "I am going to see this woman," he said, quietly. "You need not think of going with me, aunty, unless you care to. I will go alone."

"Do you think I shall let you go alone?" replied Miss Ludington, in a voice which she steadied with difficulty. "Am I not as much concerned as you are, Paul?"

"Where does this Mrs. Legrand live?" Paul asked Mrs. Slater.

"I really can't tell you that, Mr. De Riemer," she said. "It was sometime ago that I attended the seance I spoke of, and all I recall is that it was somewhere in the lower part of the city, on the east side of the Broadway, if I am not mistaken."

"Perhaps you could ascertain her address from the friend of whom you spoke, if it would not be too much trouble?" suggested Miss Ludington.

"I might do that," assented Mrs. Slater. "If she still goes to the seances she would know it. But these mediums don't generally stay long in one place, and it is quite possible that this Mrs. Legrand may not be in the city now, But if I can get her address for you I will. And now, my dear, as I am rather tired after our walk about the village, and probably you are too, will I go to my room."

CHAPTER V.

Mrs. Slater went away the next morning. On the following day but one Miss Ludington received a letter from her. She told her friend how glad she was that she had not postponed her visit to her, for if she had set it for a single day later she could not have made it at all. When she returned home she found that her husband had received an offer of a lucrative business position in Cincinnati, contingent on his immediate removal there.

They had been in a whirl of packing ever since, and were to take that night's train for Cincinnati, and whether they ever again came East to live was very doubtful. In a postscript, written crosswise, she said:

"I have been in such a rush ever since I came home that I declare I had clean forgotten till this moment about my promise to hunt up Mrs. Legrand's address for you. Very likely you have also forgotten by this time our talk about her, and if so it will not matter. But it vexes me to fail in a promise, and, if possible, I will snatch a moment before we leave to send a note to the friend I spoke of, and ask her to look the woman up for you."

Instead of being disappointed, Miss Ludington was, on the whole, relieved to get this letter, and inclined to hope that Mrs. Slater had failed to find the time to write her friend. In that case this extraordinary project of visiting a spiritualist medium would quietly fall through, which was the best thing that could happen.

The fact is, after sleeping on it, she had seen clearly that such a proceeding for a person of her position and antecedents would not only be preposterous, but almost disreputable. She was astonished at herself to think that her feelings could have been so wrought upon as to cause her seriously to contemplate such a step. All her life she had held the conviction, which she supposed to be shared by all persons of culture and respectability, that spiritualism was a low and immoral superstition, invariably implying fraud in its professors, and folly in its dupes: something, in fact, quite below the notice of persons of intelligence or good taste. As for the idea that this medium could show her the spirit of her former self, or any other real spirit, it was simply imbecile to entertain it for a moment.

If, however, Miss Ludington was relieved by Mrs. Slater's letter, Paul was keenly disappointed. His prejudice against spiritualism was by no means so deeply rooted as hers. In a general way he had always believed mediums to be frauds, and their shows mere shams, but he had been ready to allow with Mrs. Slater, that, mixed up in all this fraud, there might be a very little truth.

His mind admitted a bare possibility that this Mrs. Legrand might be able to show him the living face and form of his spirit-love. That possibility once admitted had completely dominated his imagination, and it made little difference whether it was one chance in a thousand or one in a million. He was like the victim of the lottery mania, whose absorption in contemplating the possibility of drawing the prize renders him quite oblivious of the nine hundred and ninety-nine blank tickets.

Previous to Mrs. Slater's visit he had been quite content in his devotion to an ideal mistress, for the reason that any nearer approach to her had not occurred to him as a possibility. But now the suggestion that he might see her face to face had so inflamed his imagination that it was out of the question for him to regain his former serenity. He resolved that, in case they should fail to hear from Mrs. Slater's friend, he would set about finding Mrs. Legrand himself, or, failing that, would go to some other medium. There would be no solace for the fever that had now got into his blood, until experiment should justify his daring hope, or prove it baseless.

However, the third day after Mrs. Slater's letter there came one from her friend, Mrs. Rhinehart. She said that she had received a note from Mrs. Slater, who had suddenly been called to Cincinnati, telling that Miss Ludington desired the address of Mrs. Legrand, with a view to securing a private seance. She could have sent the address at once, as she had it; but Mrs. Legrand was so overrun with business that an application to her by letter, especially from a stranger like Miss Ludington, might not have any result. And so Mrs. Rhinehart, who had been only too happy to oblige any friend of Mrs. Slater's, had called personally upon Mrs. Legrand to arrange for the seance. The medium had told her at first that she was full of previous engagements for a month ahead, and that it would be impossible to give Miss Ludington a seance. When, however, Mrs. Rhinehart told her that Miss Ludington's purpose in asking for the seance was to test the question whether our past selves have immortal souls distinct from our present selves, Mrs. Legrand became greatly interested, and at once said that she would cancel a previous appointment, and give Miss Ludington a seance the following evening, at her parlours, No. -- East Tenth Street, at nine o'clock. Mrs. Legrand had said that while she had never heard a belief in the immortality of past selves avowed, there had not been lacking in her relations with the spirit-world some mysterious experiences that seemed to confirm it. She should, therefore, look forward to the issue of the experiment the following evening with nearly as much confidence, and quite as much interest, as Miss Ludington herself. Mrs. Rhinehart hoped that the following evening would be convenient for Miss Ludington. She had assumed the responsibility of making the engagement positive, as she might have failed in securing a seance altogether had she waited to communicate with Miss Ludington. Hoping that "the conditions would be favourable," she remained, &c. &c.

When Miss Ludington had read this letter to Paul, she intimated, though rather faintly, that it was still not too late to withdraw from the enterprise; they could send Mrs. Legrand her fee, say that it was not convenient for them to come on the evening fixed, and so let the matter drop. Paul stared at her in astonishment, and said that, if she did not feel like going, he would go alone, as he had at first proposed. Upon this Miss Ludington once more declared that they would go together, and said nothing further about sacrificing the appointment.

The fact is she did not really wish to sacrifice it. She was experiencing a revulsion of feeling; Mrs. Rhinehart's letter had affected her almost as strongly as Mrs. Slater's talk. The fact that Mrs. Legrand had at once seen the reasonableness and probability of the belief in the immortality of past selves made it difficult for Miss Ludington to think of her as a mere vulgar impostor. The vague hint of the medium's as to strange experiences with the spirit world, confirmatory of this belief, appealed to her imagination in a powerful manner. Of what description might the mysterious monitions be, which, coming to this woman in the dim between-world where she groped, had prepared her to accept as true, on its first statement, a belief that to others seemed so hard to credit? What clutchings of spirit fingers in the dark! What moanings of souls whom no one recognised!

The confidence which Mrs. Legrand had expressed that the seance would prove a success affected Miss Ludington very powerfully. It impressed her as the judgment of an expert; it compelled her to recognize not only as possible, but even as probable, that, on the evening of the following day, she should behold the beautiful girl whom once, so many years before, she had called herself; for so at best would words express this wonder.

With a trembling ecstasy, which in vain she tried to reason down, she began to prepare herself for the presence of one fresh from the face of God and the awful precincts of eternity.

As for Paul, there was no conflict of feeling with prejudice in his case; he gave himself wholly up to a delirious expectation. How would his immortal mistress look? How would she move? What would be her stature--what her bearing? How would she gaze upon him? If not with love he should die at her feet. If with love how should he bear it?

Mrs. Rhinehart's letter had been received in the morning, and during the rest of the day Miss Ludington and Paul seemed quite to forget each other in their absorption in the thoughts suggested by the approaching event. They sat abstracted and silent at table, and, on rising, went each their own way. In the exalted state of their imaginations the enterprise they had in hand would not bear talking over.

When she retired to bed Miss Ludington found that sleep was out of the question. About two o'clock in the morning she heard Paul leave his room and go downstairs. Putting on dressing-gown and slippers she softly followed him. There was a light in the sitting-room and the door was ajar. Stepping noiselessly to it she looked in.

Paul was standing before, the fireplace, leaning on the mantelpiece, and looking up into the eyes of the girl above, smiling and talking softly to her, Miss Ludington entered the room and laid her hand gently on his arm. Her appearance did not seem to startle him in the least. "Paul, my dear boy!" she said, "you had better go to bed."

"It's no use," he said; "I can't sleep, and I had to come down here and look at her. Think, just think, aunty, that to-morrow we shall see her."

The young fellow's nervous excitement culminated in a burst of ecstatic tears, and soon afterwards Miss Ludington induced him to go to bed.

How much more he loved the girl than even she did! She was filled with dread as she thought of the effect which a disappointment of the hope he had given himself up to might produce. And what folly, after all, it was to expect anything but disappointment!

The spectacle of Paul's fatuous confidence had taken hers away.

CHAPTER VI

As the drive over to East Tenth Street was a long one, the carriage had been ordered at seven o'clock, and soon after tea, of which neither Miss Ludington nor Paul had been able to take a mouthful, they set out.

"I am afraid we are doing something very wrong and foolish," said Miss Ludington, feebly, as the carriage rolled down the village street.

During the drive of nearly two hours not another word was said.

The carriage at length drew up before the house in Tenth Street. It stood in a brick block, and there was no sign of the business pursued within, except a small white card on the door bearing the words, "Mrs. Legrand. Materializing, Business, and Test Medium. Clairvoyant."

An old-looking little girl of ten or twelve years of age opened the door. The child's big black eyes, and long snaky locks falling about a pale face, gave her an elfish look quite in keeping with the character of the house. She at once ushered the callers into the front parlour, where a lady and gentleman were sitting, who proved to be Mrs. Legrand and her manager and man of business, Dr. Hull.

The latter was a tall person, of highly respectable and even imposing appearance, to which a high forehead, a pair of gold-bowed spectacles, and a long white beard considerably added. He looked like a scholar, and his speech was that of a man of education.

Mrs. Legrand was a large woman, with black hair sprinkled with grey and worn short like a man's. She had a swarthy complexion, and her eyes were surrounded by noticeably large dark rings, giving an appearance of wretched ill-health. Her manner was extremely languid, as of a person suffering from nervous exhaustion. She kept her eyes half shut, and spoke as if with an effort.

"Did Mrs. Rhinehart tell you," she said to Miss Ludington, "of the interest which I feel in your theory, that the souls of our past selves exist in spirit-land? If my seance to-night realizes your expectations, spirit science will have taken a great step forward."

"My conviction will remain the same whatever the result may be to night," said Miss Ludington.

"I am glad to hear you say so," replied Mrs. Legrand languidly; "but I feel that we shall be successful, and my intuitions rarely deceive me."

A trembling came over Paul at these words.

There was a little more general conversation, and the silence which followed was interrupted by Dr. Hull.

"I suppose there is no reason why the seance should not proceed, Mrs. Legrand?"

"I know of none," assented that lady in lifeless tones. "Please show our friends the cabinet."

Dr. Hull rose. "It is usual," he said, "for those who attend our seances to be asked to satisfy themselves that deception is impossible by an examination of the apartment which Mrs. Legrand occupies during her trance, and from which the materialized spirit appears. Will you kindly step this way?"

The room in which they sat was a long apartment, divided by double sliding-doors into a front and back parlour, the former of which had been the scene of the preceding conversation.

Dr. Hull now conducted the two visitors into the back parlour, which proved to be of similar size and appearance to the front parlour, except that it contained no furniture whatever. There was only one window in the back parlour, and this was firmly closed by inside blinds.

It was also uncurtained, and in plain view from the front parlour. Besides the connection with the front parlour, there was but one door in the back parlour. This opened into a small apartment, about six feet by five, which had been taken out of the right-hand rear corner of the back parlour, and was separated from it by a partition reaching to the ceiling. This was the cabinet. It had neither window nor door, except the one into the back parlour. A sofa was its only article of furniture, and this was of wicker-work, so that nothing could be concealed beneath it.

"Mrs. Legrand lies upon this sofa while in a state of trance, during which the spirit is materialized, and appears to us," explained Dr. Hull.

A rug lay on the floor of the cabinet, the walls were of hard-finished white plaster, quite bare, and the ceiling, like that of the parlours, was plain white, without ornament.

There seemed no possibility of introducing any person into the cabinet or the back parlour without the knowledge of those in the front parlour. But Dr. Hull insisted upon making assurance doubly sure by pounding upon the walls and pulling up the rug in the cabinet, to prove that no sliding panel or trap-door trick was possible. There was something calculated to make an unbeliever very uneasy in the quiet confidence of these people, and the business-like way in which they went to work to make it impossible to account for any phenomenon that might appear, on any other but a supernatural theory. No doubt whatever now remained in the mind of Miss Ludington or Paul that the wonderful mystery which they had hardly dared to dream of was about to be enacted before them. They followed Dr. Hull on his tour of inspection as if they were in a dream, mechanically observing what he pointed out, but replying at random to his remarks, and, indeed, barely aware of what they were doing. The sense of the unspeakably awful and tender scene so soon to pass before their eyes absorbed every susceptibility of their minds.

Nor indeed would this detective work have had any interest for them in any case. They would have been willing to concede the medium all the machinery she desired. There was no danger that they could be deceived as to the reality of the face and form that for so many years had been enshrined in their memories.

There might be as many side entrances to the cabinet as desired, but she whom they looked for could come only from the spirit-land.

The front parlour, too, having been investigated, to show the impossibility of any person's being concealed there, Dr. Hull proceeded to close and lock the hall-door, that being the only exit connecting this suite of rooms with the rest of the house. Having placed a heavy chair against the locked door for further security, he gave the key to Paul.

Mrs. Legrand now rose, and without a word to any one passed through the back parlour and disappeared in the cabinet.

As she did so a wild desire to fly from the room and the house came over Miss Ludington. Not that she did not long inexpressibly to see the vision that was drawing near, whose beautiful feet might even now be on the threshold, but the sense of its awfulness overcame her. She felt that she was not fit, not ready, for it now. If she could only have more time to prepare herself, and then could come again. But it was too late to draw back.

Dr. Hull had arranged three chairs across the broad doorway between the back and front parlours, and facing the former. He asked Miss Ludington to occupy the middle chair, and, trembling in every limb, she did so. Paul took the chair by her side, the other being apparently for Dr. Hull.

The elfish little girl, whom they called Alta, and who appeared to be the daughter of Mrs. Legrand, meanwhile took her place at a piano standing in the front parlour.

All being now ready, Dr. Hull proceeded to turn the gas in the two parlours very low. The jets in both rooms were controlled by a stop-cock in the wall by the side of the doorway between them. There were two jets in the back parlour, fastened to the wall dividing it from the front parlour, one on each side of the door, so as to throw light on any figure coming out of the cabinet. The light they diffused, after being turned down; was enough to render forms and faces sufficiently visible for the recognition of acquaintances, though a close study of features would have been difficult.

It now appeared that the glass shades of the jets in the back parlour were of a bluish tint, which lent a peculiarly weird effect to the illumination.

Dr. Hull now took the remaining chair by Miss Ludington's side, and a perfect silence of some moments ensued, during which she could perfectly hear the beating of Paul's heart. Then Alta began, with a wonderfully soft touch, to play a succession of low, dreamy chords, rather than any set composition--music that thrilled the listeners with vague suggestions of the unfathomable mystery and unutterable sadness of human life. She played on and on. It seemed to two of the hearers that she played for hours, although it was probably but a few minutes.

At last the music flowed slower, trickled, fell in drops, and ceased.

They had a sensation of being breathed upon by a faint, cool draught of air, and then appeared in the door-way of the cabinet the figure of a beautiful girl, which, after standing still a moment, glided forth, by an imperceptible motion, into the room.

The light, which had before seemed so faint, now proved sufficient to bring out every line of her face and form. Or was it that the figure itself was luminous by some light from within?

Paul heard Miss Ludington gasp; but if he had known that she was dying he could not have taken his eyes from the apparition.

For it was Ida who stood before him; no counterfeit of the painter now, but radiant with life.

Her costume was exactly that of her picture, white, with a low bodice; but how utterly had the artist failed to reproduce the ravishing contours of her young form, the enchanting sweetness of her expression. The golden hair fell in luxuriant tresses about the face and down the dazzling shoulders. The lips were parted in a pleased smile as, with a gliding motion, she approached the rapt watchers.

Her eyes rested on Miss Ludington with a look full of recognition and a tenderness that seemed beyond the power of mortal eyes to express.

Then she looked at Paul. Her smile was no longer the smile of an angel, but of a woman. The light of her violet eyes burned like delicious flame to the marrow of his bones.

She was so near him that he could have touched her. Her beauty overcame his senses. Forgetting all else, in an agony of love, he was about to clasp her in his arms, but she drew back with a gentle gesture of denial.

Then a sudden and indescribable wavering passed over her face, like the passing of the wind over a field of rye, and slowly, as if reluctantly obeying an unseen attraction, she retreated, still facing them, across the room, and disappeared within the cabinet.

Instantly Alta touched the piano, playing the same slow, heavy chords as before. But this time she played but a few moments, and when she ceased, Mrs. Legrand's voice was heard faintly calling her. She glided between the chairs in the door-way and entered the cabinet, drawing a ***portiere*** across its door behind her.

As she did so, Dr. Hull touched the stopcock in the wall by his side, turning on the gas in both parlours, and proceeded to unlock and open the hall-door.

"It was the most successful seance I have ever witnessed," he said. "The conditions must have been unusually favourable. How were you pleased, Miss Ludington?"

The abrupt transition from the shadows of the between-world to the glare of gas-light, from the communion of spirits to the brisk business-like tones of Dr. Hull, was quite too much for the poor lady, and with a piteous gesture, she buried her face in her hands. Alta now came out of the cabinet, and said that her mother would like them to examine it once more.

Miss Ludington took no notice of the request, but Paul, who had continued to sit staring into vacancy, as if for him the seance were still going on, sprang up at Alta's invitation and accepted it with alacrity. The eagerness with which he peered into the corner of the cabinet, and the disappointment which his face showed when he perceived no trace of any person there save Mrs. Legrand and Alta, might naturally have suggested to them that he suspected fraud; but the fact was very different. His conduct was merely the result of a confused hope that he might gain another glimpse of Ida by following her to the place within which she had vanished.

When Paul looked into the cabinet, Mrs. Legrand was lying upon the lounge, and Alta was administering smelling salts to her. As he turned away disappointed, the medium rose, and leaning on her daughter, returned to the front parlour. She looked completely overcome. Her face was deathly pale, and the dark rings around her eyes were larger and darker than ever. She leaned back in her chair, which had a special rest for her head, and closed her eyes.

As neither Dr. Hull nor Alta showed any surprise at her condition, it was apparently the ordinary result of a seance.

To her faint inquiry whether the materialization had been satisfactory to Miss Ludington, the latter replied that it had been all, and more than all, she had dared dream of. Dr. Hull, in a very enthusiastic manner, went on to describe the manifestation more particularly. He declared that the present evening a new world of spirit-life had been revealed, and a new era in spiritualism had opened.

"I have been devoted to the study of spiritualism for thirty years," he exclaimed; "but I have never been present at so wonderful a seance as this. I grow dizzy when I think of the field of speculation which it opens up. The spirits of our past selves--? And yet why not, why not? Like all great discoveries it seems most simple when once brought to light. It accounts, no doubt, for the throng of unknown spirits of which mediums are so often conscious, and for the many materializations and communications which no one recognizes."

Meanwhile the wretched appearance of the medium aroused Miss Ludington's sympathies, in spite of the distracted condition of her mind.

"Is Mrs. Legrand always prostrated in this manner after a seance?" she asked.

Dr. Hull answered for the medium. "Not generally quite so much so," he said; "the strain on her vitality is always very trying, but it is especially so when a new spirit materializes, as to-night. Out of her being, somehow, and just how, I know no better than you, is woven the veil of seeming flesh, yes, and even the clothing which the spirit assumes in order to appear. The fact that Mrs. Legrand suffers from heart disease makes seances not only more exhausting for her than for other mediums, but really dangerous. I have told her, as a physician, and other physicians have told her, that she is liable at any time to die in a trance."

Paul now spoke for the first time since the conclusion of the seance. "What do you fancy would be the effect on the spirit if a medium should die during a materialization, as you have supposed?" he inquired.

"That can only be a matter of theory," replied Dr. Hull; "the accident has never happened."

"But it might happen."

"Yes, it might happen."

"Is not the spirit as much dependent on the medium for dematerializing and resuming the spirit-form, as for materializing?" asked Paul.

"I see what you mean," said Dr. Hull. "You think that in case the medium should die during a materialization, the spirit might be left in a materialized state. How does it strike you, Mrs. Legrand?"

"I don't know," replied that lady, with her eyes closed. "Spirits require our aid as much to lay aside their bodies as to assume them. If the medium died meantime, I should think that the spirit might find some trouble in dematerializing."

"Is it not possible," said Paul, "that it might be unable to dematerialize at all? Would not the medium's death close against it the only door by which it could return to the spirit-world, shutting it out in this life with us henceforth? More than that: would not the already materialized spirit be in a position to succeed to the physical life which the medium relinquished? Already possessed of a part of the medium's vitality, would not the remainder naturally flow to it when given up in death, and thus complete its materialization?"

"And give it an earthly body like ours?" exclaimed Miss Ludington.

"Yes, like ours," replied Paul. "I suppose it would simply take up its former life on earth where it had been left off, ceasing to possess a spirit's powers, and knowing only what and whom it knew at the point when its first life on earth had ceased."

"After what I have seen to-night, nothing will ever seem impossible to me again," said Miss Ludington.

"As Miss Ludington suggests," observed Dr. Hull, "in spiritualism one soon ceases to consider whether a thing be wonderful or not, but only if it be true. And so as to this matter. Now, if the death of a medium should be absolutely instantaneous, the spirit might, indeed, be unable to dematerialize, and might even succeed to the medium's earth life, as you suggest. The trouble with the theory--and it seems to me a fatal one--is, that death is almost never, if indeed it is ever, absolutely instantaneous but only comparatively so; and it seems to me that the least possible interval of time would be sufficient to enable the spirit to dematerialize. Consequently, it strikes me, that while the result you suppose is theoretically possible, it could, practically, never occur. Still, the subject is one of mere conjecture at most, and one opinion is, perhaps, as good as another."

"I think you are probably right," said Paul; "it was only a fancy I had."

"Why does Mrs. Legrand persist in giving seances if she is not in a fit condition?" said Miss Ludington.

"Well," replied Dr. Hull, "you see we spiritualists do not regard death as so serious a matter as do many others. Our mediums, especially, who stand with one hand clasped by spirits and the other by mortals, are almost indifferent which way they are drawn; besides, you see, she is recognized as the most fully developed medium in the United States to-day, and many spirits, which cannot materialize through other mediums, are dependent upon her; she feels that she has a duty to discharge towards the spirit-world, at whatever risk to herself. I doubt if to-night's seance, for example, would have been successful with any other medium."

Immediately after this conversation Miss Ludington and Paul took their departure. Dr. Hull went, out with them to the carriage, and was obliged to remind them of the little matter of Mrs. Legrand's fee, which they had entirely forgotten.

CHAPTER VII.

Now, before she ever had heard of Mrs. Legrand, Miss Ludington had fully believed that her former self had an immortal existence, apart and distinct from her present self, and Paul, to whom she was indebted for this belief, held it even more firmly than she.

But there is a great difference between the strongest form of faith and the absolute assurance of sight. The effect of the vision which they had witnessed in Mrs. Legrand's parlours was almost as startling as if they had not expected to see it.

Very little was said in the carriage going home, but, as they were crossing the ferry, Miss Ludington exclaimed, in an awestruck voice,

"O Paul! was it not strange!"

"Strange? Strange?" he echoed, in strong, exultant tones. "How oddly you use the word, aunty! You might well say how strange, if we mortals were isolated here on this little island of time, with no communication with the mainland of eternity; but how can you call it strange when you find out that we are not isolated? Surely it is not strange, but supremely reasonable, right, and natural."

"I suppose it is so," said Miss Ludington, "but if I had let you go alone to-night, and stayed at home, I could never have fully believed you when you told me what you had seen any more than I shall ever expect any one to believe me. Think, Paul, if I had not gone, if I had not seen her, if she had not given me that look! I knew, of course, if she appeared that I should recognize her, but I did not dare to be sure that she would recognize me. I remember her, but she never saw me on earth."

"It was as a spirit that she knew you, and that is the way she knew me, and knew that I loved her," said Paul, with a sudden huskiness in his voice.

"Surely that makes it clear," said Miss Ludington, "that the spirits of our past selves love us who follow them, as we, in looking back, yearn after them, and not merely await us at the end, but are permitted to watch over us as we complete the journey which they began. I am sure that if people knew this they would never feel lonely or forlorn again."

It was a relief to Paul when they reached home and he could be alone.

In an ecstasy of happiness that was like a delicious pain, he sat till morning in his unlighted chamber, gazing into the darkness with a set smile, motionless, and breathing only by deep, infrequent inhalations. What were the joys of mortal love to the transports that were his? What were the smoky fires of earthly passion to his pure, keen flame, almost too strong for a heart of flesh to bear?

As he strove to realize what it was to be beloved by an immortal, the veil between time and eternity was melted by the hot breath of his passion, and the confines of the natural and the supernatural were confounded.

As the east grew light he began to feel the weariness of the intense mental strain which had led up to, and culminated in, the transcendent experience of the previous evening. A tranquil happiness succeeded his exalted mood, and, lying down, he slept soundly till noon, when he went downstairs to find Miss Ludington anxiously waiting for him to reassure her that her recollection of the last night was not altogether a dream, as she had half convinced herself since waking.

Paul had to go into Brooklyn to do some business for Miss Ludington that day, but the men he dealt with seemed to him shadows.

After finishing with them he went over to New York, and presently found himself on East Tenth Street. He had not intended to go there. His feet had borne him involuntarily to the spot. He could not resist the temptation of drawing near to the place where she had been only a few hours before. He walked to and fro before Mrs. Legrand's house for an hour, and then stood a long time on the opposite side, looking at the closed windows of the front parlour, quite unconscious that he had become an object of curiosity to numerous persons in adjoining houses, and of marked suspicion to the policeman at the corner.

Finally he crossed the street, mounted the steps, and rang the bell. The door was opened, after a considerable interval, by Alta, the elfish little girl. Paul asked for Mrs. Legrand. Alta said that her mother was ill to-day, and not able to see any one. Paul then asked for Dr. Hull. He was not in.

"I wanted to arrange for another seance," he said.

"Will you write, or will you call to-morrow?" asked Alta, in a business-like manner.

Paul said he would call. Then he hesitated.

"Excuse me," he said, "but may I ask you if there is any one now in the parlour where we were last night?"

"No one is there," replied the little girl.

"Could you let me just go in and see where she was?" asked Paul, humbly. "I would not keep you a moment."

Alta, in her character of door-keeper to this house of mystery, was, doubtless, in the habit of seeing queer people, bent on queer errands. She merely asked him to step within the hall, saying that she would speak to her mother. Presently she returned with the desired permission, and, producing a key, unlocked the parlour door, and ushered Paul in.

It was late in the afternoon, and the heavy curtains and blinds left the rooms almost dark. There was barely light enough to see that all was just as it had been the night before. The sounds of the street penetrated the closed apartments but faintly. With the step of one on holy ground, Paul advanced to the spot where he had been seated when the vision appeared to him the night before.

Aided by the darkness, the silence, and by the identity of the surroundings, the memory of that vision returned to him as he stood there with a vividness which, in the overwrought condition of his nerves, it was impossible for him to distinguish from reality. Once more a radiant figure glided noiselessly from the cabinet, which was darkly outlined in the corner of the room, and stood before him. Once more her eyes burned on his, until, forgetting all but her beauty, he put forth his arms to clasp her. A startled exclamation from Alta banished the vision, and he perceived that he was smiling upon the empty air.

He went away from the house ecstatically happy. He believed that he had really seen her. He had no doubt that, aided by the mediumship of love, she had actually appeared to him a second time in a form only a little less material than the night before.

Of this experience he did not tell Miss Ludington. This interview, which Ida had granted to him alone, he kept as a precious secret.

The next day, as he had promised, Paul called at Mrs. Legrand's and saw Dr.

Hull. That gentleman was unable to promise him anything definite about a seance, on account of Mrs. Legrand's continued illness.

"Is she seriously sick?" asked Paul, with a new terror.

"I think not," said Dr. Hull; "but her trouble is of the heart, the result of the nervous crises which a trance medium is necessarily subject to, and a disease of the heart may at any time take an unexpected turn."

"Has she the best advice?" asked Paul. "Excuse me; but if she has not, and if her pecuniary means do not enable her to afford it, I beg you will let me secure it for her."

Dr. Hull thanked him, but said that he was a physician himself, and that, on account of his acquaintance with her constitutional peculiarities, Mrs. Legrand considered him, and he considered himself, better able to treat her than any strange physician. "You seem to be very much interested in her case," added the doctor, with a slight intonation of surprise.

"Can you wonder?" replied Paul. "Is she not door-keeper between this world and the world of spirits where my love is? Don't think me brutal if I confess to you that what I think of most is that her death might close that door."

"I do not think you brutal," replied Dr. Hull; "what you feel is very natural."

"Is it not strange--is it not hard to bear," cried Paul, giving way to his feelings, "that the key of the gate between the world of spirits and of men should be intrusted to a weak and sickly woman?"

"It is hard to bear, no doubt," replied Dr. Hull; "but it is not strange. It is in accordance with the laws by which this world has always been conducted. From the beginning has not the power of calling spirits out of the unknown into this earth life been intrusted to weak and sickly women? What the world loosely calls spiritualism is no isolated phenomenon or set of phenomena. The universe is spiritual. Much as we claim for our mediums, the mediumship of motherhood is far more marvellous. Our mediums can enable spirits already alive, and able by their own wills to cooperate, to pass before our eyes for a moment. To hold them longer in our view exceeds their power. But these other women, these mothers, call souls out of nothingness, and clothe them with bodies, so that they speak, walk, work, love, and hate, some forty, some fifty, some seventy years."

"You are right," said Paul bowing his head. "It is not strange though it is hard to bear."

The effect of the seance at Mrs. Legrand's upon Miss Ludington had been far less disturbing than upon Paul. To her it had been a lofty spiritual consolation, setting the seal of absolute assurance upon a faith that had been before too great, too strange, too beautiful for her to fully realize.

When Paul brought word that Mrs. Legrand was sick and might die, and that if she died that first vision of Ida might also prove the last to be vouchsafed them on earth, although she was deeply grieved, yet the thought did not seem so intolerable to her as to him. She had, indeed, hoped that from time to time she should see Ida again; still, her life was mostly past, and it was chiefly upon the communion they would enjoy in heaven, not momentary and imperfect as here, but perennial and complete, that her heart was set.

Very different was it with Paul. He was young; heaven was very far off, and the way thither, unless cheered by occasional visitations of his radiant mistress, seemed inexpressibly long and dreary. The nature of his sentiment for Ida had changed since he had seen her clothed in a living form, from the worship of a sweet but dim ideal to the passion which a living woman inspires. He thought of her no more as a spirit, lofty and serene, but as a beautiful maiden with the love-light in her eyes.

He was not able to find his former inspiration in the picture above the fireplace. Its still enchantment was gone. The set smile, that had ever before seemed so sweet, palled upon him. The eyes, that had always been so tender, now lacked expression. The lips that the boy had climbed up to kiss, how had the artist failed to intimate their exquisite curves! The whole picture had suffered a subtle deterioration, and looked hard, wooden, lifeless, and almost, unlike. The living woman had eclipsed the portrait. Fortunate it is for the fame of painters that their originals do not oftener return to earth.

If Mrs. Legrand had been his own mother Paul could not have been more assiduous in his calls and inquiries as to her condition, nor could his relief have been greater when, a few days later, Dr. Hull told him that the case had taken a favourable turn, and according to her previous experience with such attacks, she would probably be as well as usual by the following day. Dr. Hull said that she had heard of Paul's frequent inquiries for her, and while she did not flatter herself that his interest in her was wholly on her own account, she was, nevertheless, so far grateful that she would give him the first seance which she was able to hold, and that would be, if she continued to improve, on the following evening.

CHAPTER VIII.

I f Miss Ludington's desire for another glimpse of Ida had lacked the passionate intensity of Paul's, she had, notwithstanding, longed for it very ardently, and when at nine o'clock the next night the carriage drew up before Mrs. Legrand's door, she was in a transport of sweet anticipation.

As for Paul he had dressed himself with extreme care for the occasion, and looked to his best advantage. He had said to himself, "Shall I not show her as much observance as I would pay to a living woman?" And who can say--for very odd, sometimes, are the inarticulate processes of the mind--that there was not at the bottom of his thoughts something of the universal lover's willingness to let his mistress see him at his best?

They found the front parlour occupied as before by Mrs. Legrand and Dr. Hull, when Alta showed them in. The medium was, as previously, the picture of ill-health, and if she did not look noticeably worse than before her sickness, it was merely because she had looked as badly as possible then. In response to inquiries about her health she admitted that she did not really feel equal to resuming her seances quite so soon, and but for disliking to disappoint them would have postponed this evening's appointment. Dr. Hull had, indeed, urged her to do so.

"You must not think of giving a seance if there is any risk of injury to your health," said Miss Ludington, though not without being sensible of a pang of disappointment. "We could not think of letting you do that, could we, Paul?"

Paul's reply to this humane suggestion was not so prompt as it should have been. In his heart he felt at that moment that he was as bad as a murderer. He knew that he was willing this woman should risk not only her health, but even her life, rather than that he should fail to see Ida. He was striving to repress this feeling, so far at least as to say that he would not insist upon going on with the seance, when

Mrs. Legrand, with a glance through her half-shut eyelids, intimating that she perfectly understood his thoughts, said, in a tone which put an end to the discussion, "Excuse me, but I shall certainly give the seance. I am much obliged for your interest in me; but I am rather notional about keeping my promises, and it is a peculiarity in which my friends have to indulge in. I daresay I shall be none the worse for the exertion."

"Doctor," she added, "will you allow our friends to inspect the cabinet?"

"That is quite needless," said Paul.

"Our friends are often willing to waive an inspection," replied Dr. Hull. "We are grateful for the confidence shown, but, in justice to ourselves, as well as for their own more absolute assurance, we always insist upon it. Otherwise, suspicions of fraud not entertained, perhaps, at the time, might afterwards occur to the mind, or be suggested by others, to which they would have no conclusive answer."

Upon this Miss Ludington and Paul permitted themselves to be conducted upon the same tour of inspection that they had made the former evening. They found everything precisely as it had been on that occasion. There was no possibility of concealing any person in the cabinet or the back parlour, and no apparent or conceivable means by which any person could reach those apartments, except through the front parlour.

On their return to the latter apartment the proceedings followed the order observed at the previous seance. Mrs. Legrand rose from her chair and walked feebly through the back parlour into the cabinet. Dr. Hull then locked and braced a chair against the door opening into the hall, giving the key to Paul. Then, having arranged the three chairs as before, across the double door between the parlours, he seated Miss Ludington and Paul, and, having turned the gas down, took the third chair.

All being ready, Alta, who was at the piano, struck the opening chords of the same soft, low music that she had played at the previous seance.

It seemed to Miss Ludington that she played much longer than before, and she began to think that either there was to be some failure in the seance, or that something had happened to Mrs. Legrand.

Perhaps she was dead. This horrible thought, added to the strain of expectancy, affected her nerves so that in another moment she must have screamed out, when, as before, she felt a faint, cool air fan her forehead, and a few seconds later Ida appeared at the door of the cabinet and glided into the room.

She was dressed as at her former appearance, in white, with her shoulders bare, and the wealth of her golden hair falling to her waist behind.

From the moment that she emerged from the shadows of the cabinet Paul's eyes were glued to her face with an intensity quite beyond any ordinary terms of description.

Fancy having not over a minute in which to photograph upon the mind a form the recollection of which is to furnish the consolation of a lifetime. The difficulties of securing this second seance, and the doubt that involved the obtaining of another, had deeply impressed him. He might never again see Ida on earth, and upon the fidelity with which his memory retained every feature of her face, every line of her figure, his thoughts by day, and his dreams by night, might have to depend for their texture until he should meet her in another world.

The lingering looks that are the lover's luxury were not for these fleeting seconds. His gaze burned upon her face and played around her form like lightning. He grudged the instantaneous muscles of the eye the time they took to make the circuit of her figure.

But when, as on that other night, she came close up to him and smiled upon him, time and circumstance were instantly forgotten, and he fell into a state of enchantment in which will and thought were inert.

He was aroused from it by an extraordinary change that came over her. She started and shivered slightly in every limb. The recognition faded out of her eyes and gave place to a blank bewilderment.

Then came a turning of her head from side to side, while, with dilated eyes, she explored the dim recesses of the room with the startled expression of an awakened sleep-walker. She half turned toward the cabinet and made an undecided movement in that direction, and then, as if the invisible cord that drew her thither had broken, she wavered, stopped, and seemed to drift toward the opposite corner of the room.

At that moment there was a gasp from the cabinet.

Dr. Hull leaped to his feet and sprang toward it, at the same time, by a turn of the stopcock by his side, setting the gas in both rooms at full blaze.

Alta, with a loud scream, rushed after him, and Miss Ludington and Paul followed them.

The pupils of their eyes had been dilated to the utmost in order to follow the movements of the apparition in the nearly complete darkness, and the first effect of the sudden blaze of gaslight was to dazzle them so completely that they had actually to grope their way to the cabinet.

The scene in the little apartment of the medium was a heartrending one.

Mrs. Legrand's body and lower limbs lay on the sofa, which was the only article of furniture, and Dr. Hull was in the act of lifting her head from the floor to which it had fallen. Her eyes were half open, and the black rings around them showed with ghastly plainness against the awful pallor which the rest of her face had taken on. One hand was clenched. The other was clutching her bodice, as if in the act of tearing it open. A little foam flecked the blue lips.

Alta threw herself upon her mother's body, sobbing, "Oh, mamma, wake up! do! do!"

"Is she dead?" asked Miss Ludington, in horrified accents.

"I don't know; I fear so. I warned her; I told her it would come. But she would do it," cried the doctor incoherently, as he tried to feel her pulse with one hand while he tore at the fastenings of her dress with the other. He set Paul at work chafing the hands of the unconscious woman, while Miss Ludington sprinkled her face and chest with ice-water from a small pitcher that stood in a corner of the cabinet, and the doctor himself endeavoured in vain to force some of the contents of a vial through her clenched teeth. "It is of no use," he said, finally; "she is past help--she is dead!"

At this Miss Ludington and Paul stood aside, and Alta, throwing herself upon her mother's form, burst into an agony of tears. "She was all I had," she sobbed.

"Had Mrs. Legrand friends?" asked Miss Ludington, conscience-stricken with the thought that she had indirectly been in part responsible for this terrible event.

"She had friends who will look after Alta," said Dr. Hull.

Their assistance being no longer needed, Miss Ludington and Paul turned from the sad scene and stepped forth from the cabinet into the back parlour.

The tragedy which they had just witnessed had to a great extent driven from their thoughts the events of the seance which it had broken off so abruptly. The impression left on their minds was that the spirit-form of Ida had vanished in the blinding flood of gas-light through which they had groped their way to the cabinet on hearing the death-rattle of the medium.

But now in the remotest corner of the room, towards which they had last seen the form of the spirit drifting, there stood a young girl. She was bending forward, shielding her eyes with her right hand from the flaring gas, as she peered curiously about the room, her whole attitude expressive of complete bewilderment.

It was Ida; but what a change had passed upon her! This was no pale spirit, counterfeiting for a few brief moments, with the aid of darkness, the semblance of mortal flesh, but an unmistakable daughter of earth. Her bosom was palpitating with agitation, and, instead of the lofty serenity of a spirit, her eyes expressed the trouble of a perplexed girl who is fast becoming frightened.

As Paul and Miss Ludington stepped forth from the cabinet she fixed upon them a pair of questioning eyes. There was not a particle of recognition in their expression. Presently she spoke. Her voice was a mezzo-soprano, low and sweet, but just now sharpened by an accent of apprehension.

"Where am I?" she asked.

After a moment, during which their brains reeled with an amazement so utter that they doubted the evidence of their senses--doubted even their own existence and identities, there had simultaneously flashed over the minds of Paul and Miss Ludington the explanation of what they beheld.

The prodigy, the theoretical possibility of which they had discussed after the seance of the week before, and scarcely thought of since, had come to pass. Dr. Hull had proved wrong, and Paul had proved right. A medium had died during a materialization, and the materialized spirit had succeeded to her vitality, and was alive as one of them.

It was no longer the spirit of Ida, knowing them by a spirit's intuition, which was before them, but the girl Ida Ludington, whose curious, unrecognizing glance testified to her ignorance of aught which the Hilton school-girl of forty years ago had not known.

It was with an inexpressible throb of exultation, after the stupor of their first momentary astonishment, that they comprehended the miracle by which in the moment when the hope of ever beholding Ida again had seemed taken from them, had restored her not only to their eyes, but to life. But how should they accost her, how make themselves known to her, how go about even to answer the question she had asked without terrifying her with new and deeper mysteries?

While they stood dumb, with hearts yearning toward her, but powerless to think of words with which to address her, Dr. Hull, hearing the sound of her voice, stepped out from the cabinet. At the sight of Ida he started back astounded, and Paul heard him exclaim under his breath, "I never thought of this"

Then he laid his hand on Paul's arm and said, in an agitated whisper, "You were right. It has happened as you said. My God, what can we say to her?"

Meanwhile, Ida was evidently becoming much alarmed at the strange looks bent upon her. "Perhaps, sir," she said, addressing Dr. Hull, with an appealing accent, "you will tell me how I came in this place?"

Then ensued an extraordinary scene of explanation, in which, seconding one another's efforts, striving to hit upon simpler analogies, plainer terms, Paul the doctor, and Miss Ludington sought to make clear to this waif from eternity, so strangely stranded on the shores of Time, the conditions and circumstances under which she had resumed an earthly existence.

For a while she only grew more terrified at their explanations, appearing to find them totally unintelligible, and, though her fears were gradually dissipated by the tenderness of their demeanour, her bewilderment seemed to increase. For a long time she continued to turn her face, with a pathetic expression of mental endeavour, from one to another, as they addressed her, only to shake her head slowly and sadly at last.

"I seem to have lost myself," she said, pressing her hand to her forehead. "I do not understand anything you say."

"It is a hard matter to understand," replied Dr. Hull. "Understanding will come later. Meanwhile, look in at the door of this room and you will see the body of the woman to whose life you have succeeded. Then you will believe us though you do not understand us."

As he spoke he indicated the door of the cabinet.

Ida stepped thither and looked in, recoiling with a sharp cry of horror. The terror in her face was piteous, and in a moment Miss Ludington was at her side, supporting and soothing her. Sobbing and trembling Ida submitted unresistingly to her ministrations, and even rested her head on Miss Ludington's shoulder.

The golden hair brushed the grey locks; the full bosom heaved against the shrunken breast of age; the wrinkled, scarred, and sallow face of the old woman touched the rounded cheek of the girl.

Fully as Paul believed that he had realized the essential and eternal distinction between the successive persons who constitute an individuality, he grew dizzy with the sheer wonder of the spectacle as he saw age thus consoling youth, and reflected upon the relation of these two persons to each other.

Presently Ida raised her head and said, "It may be as you say. My mind is all confused. I cannot think now. Perhaps I shall understand it better after a while."

"If you will come home with me now," said Miss Ludington, "before you sleep I will convince you what we are to each other. Will you come with me?"

"Oh, yes!" exclaimed the girl. "Let us go. Let us leave this awful place;" and she glanced with a shudder at the door of the cabinet.

A few moments later the house of death had been left behind, and Miss Ludington's carriage, with its three passengers was rolling homewards.

Before leaving, Miss Ludington had told Dr. Hull that he might command her so far as any pecuniary assistance should be needed either with reference to the funeral or in connection with providing for Alta. She said that it would be a relief to her to be allowed to do anything she could. Dr. Hull thanked her and said that, as Mrs. Legrand had friends in the city, it would probably be unnecessary to trouble her. If for no other purpose, however, he said that he should possibly communicate with her hereafter with a view to informing himself as to the future of the young lady who had that night assumed the earth-life which his dear friend, Mrs. Legrand, had laid aside.

It was an incident of this extraordinary situation that Miss Ludington found herself at disadvantage even in expressing the formal condolence she proffered. With Ida before her eyes it was impossible that she should honestly profess to deplore the event, however tragical, which had brought her back to earth. As for Paul he said nothing at all.

The rattling of the wheels on the stony pavement was enough of itself to make conversation difficult in the carriage; even if it would otherwise have flowed easily in a company so strangely assorted. As the light of the street lamps from time to time flashed in at the windows Paul saw that Ida's face continued to wear the look of helpless daze which it had assumed from the moment that the sight of the dead woman in the cabinet had convinced her that she could not trust her own knowledge as to the relations of those about her.

But when at last the carriage rolled through the gates of Miss Ludington's estate, and the houses of the mimic village began to glance by, her manner instantly changed. With an exclamation of joyful surprise, she put her head out at the window, and then looking back at them, cried, delightedly, "Why it's Hilton! You have brought me home! There's our house!" No sooner had she alighted than she ran up the walk to the door, and tried to open it. Paul, hurrying after, unlocked it, and she burst in, while he and Miss Ludington followed her, wondering.

The servants had gone to bed, leaving the lower part of the house dimly lighted. Ida hurried on ahead from room to room with the confident step of one whose feet knew every turning. It was evident that she needed no one to introduce her there.

When Miss Ludington and Paul followed her into the sitting-room, she was standing before her own picture in an attitude of utter astonishment.

"Where did they get that picture of me?" she demanded. "I never had a picture painted."

For a few moments there was no reply. Those she addressed were engrossed in comparing the portrait with its original. The resemblance was striking enough, but it was no wonder that after once seeing the living Ida, Paul had found the canvas stiff and hard and lifeless.

"No," said Miss Ludington, "you never had a picture painted. It was not till many years after you had left the world that this picture was painted. It was enlarged from this portrait of you. Do you remember it?" and taking the locket containing the ivory portrait of Ida from her neck where she had worn it so many years, she opened and gave it to the girl.

"Why, it is my ivory portrait!" exclaimed Ida. "How did you come by it? What do you mean about my leaving the world? Something strange has happened to me, I know, but did I die? I don't remember dying. Oh, can't somebody explain what has happened to me?"

The dazed look which had disappeared from her face since her recognition of the village and the homestead had come back, and her last words were a bitter cry that went to the hearts of the listeners.

Now, all the time they had been in the carriage, Paul had been trying to think of some mode of setting her relationship to Miss Ludington in a light so clear that she must comprehend it, for it was evident that the confused explanations at Mrs. Legrand's had availed little, if anything, to that end. Unless this could be done she seemed likely to remain indefinitely in this dazed mental state, which must be so exquisitely painful to her, and was scarcely less so to them.

"If you will listen to me patiently," he said, "I will try to explain. You know that some strange thing has happened to you, and you must expect to find the explanation as strange as the thing itself; but it is not hard to understand."

Ida's eyes were fixed on him with the expression of one listening for her life.

"Do you remember being a little girl of nine or ten years old?" he asked.

"Oh, yes!" she answered. "I remember that perfectly well."

"You are now a young woman," he went on. "Where is that little girl whom you remember? What has become of her?"

"Why, I don't know," replied Ida. "I suppose she is somewhere in me."

"But you don't look like a little girl, or think or act or feel like one. How can she be in you?"

"Where else could she be?" replied Ida.

"Oh, there is no lack of room for her," said Paul; "the universe is big enough for all the souls that ever lived in it. Suppose, now, you believed her to be still alive as a spirit, just as she was, still alive somewhere in the land of spirits, not transformed into the young lady that you are at all, you understand, for that would only be another way of saying that she was dead, but just as she was, a child, with a child's loves, a child's thoughts, a child's feelings, and a child's face--can you suppose such a thing, just as an effort of imagination?"

"Oh, yes!" said Ida; "I can suppose that."

"Well, then," said Paul, "suppose also that you remembered this little girl very tenderly, and longed to look on her face again, although knowing that she was a spirit now. Suppose that you went to a woman having a mysterious power to call up the spirits of the departed, and suppose that she called up the spirit of this child-self of yours, and that you recognized it, and suppose that just at that moment the woman died, and her earthly life was transferred to the spirit of the child, so that instead of being a spirit, she became again a living child, but unable to recognize you who loved her so well, because when she lived on earth, you, of course, had not yet come into existence. Suppose you brought this child home with you----"

"What do you mean?" interrupted Ida, with dilating eyes. "Am I----"

"You are to that woman," broke in Paul, indicating Miss Ludington, "what the child would have been to you. You are bound to her by the same tie by which that little girl would have been bound to you. She remembers and loves you as you would remember and love that child; but you do not know her any more than that child would know you. You both share the name of Ida Ludington, according to the usage of men as to names; but I think there is no danger of your being confounded with each other, either in your own eyes or those of lookers-on."

Ida had at last comprehended. The piercing look, expressive of mingled attraction and repulsion, which she fixed upon Miss Ludington, left no doubt of that. It implied alarm, mistrust, and something that was almost defiance, yet with hints of a possible tenderness.

It was such a look as a daughter, stolen from her cradle and grown to maidenhood among strangers, might fix upon the woman claiming to be her mother, except that not only was Miss Ludington a stranger to Ida, but the relation which she claimed to sustain to her was one that had never before been realized between living persons on earth, however it might be, in heaven.

"Do you understand?" said Paul.

"I--think--I--do. But how--strange--it is!" she replied, in lingering tones, her gaze continuing to rest, as if fascinated, upon Miss Ludington.

The latter's face expressed a great elation, an impassioned tenderness held in check through fear of terrifying its object.

"I do not wonder it seems strange," she said, very softly. "You have yet no evidence as to who I am. I remember you--oh, how well!--but you cannot remember me, nor is there any instinct answering to memory by which you can recognize me. You have a right to require that I should prove that I am what I claim to be; that I am also Ida Ludington; that I am your later self. Do not fear, my darling. I shall be able to convince you very soon."

She made Ida sit down, and then went to an ancient secretary, that stood in a corner of the room, and unlocked a drawer, the key to which she always carried on her person.

Paul remembered from the time he was a little boy seeing her open this drawer on Sunday afternoons and cry over the keepsakes which it contained.

She took out now a bundle of letters, a piece of ribbon, a locket, a bunch of faded flowers, and a few other trifles, and brought them to Ida.

Paul left the room on tiptoe. This was a scene where a third person, one might almost say a second person, would be an interloper.

When, a long time after, he returned, Miss Ludington was sitting in the chair where Ida had been sitting, smiling and crying, and the girl, with eyes that shone like stars, was bending over her, and kissing the tears away.

The night was now almost spent, and the early dawn of midsummer, peering through the windows, and already dimming the lights, warned them that the day would soon be at hand.

"You shall have your own bedroom," said Miss Ludington. The face of the old lady was flushed, and her high-pitched and tremulous voice betrayed an exhilaration like that of intoxication. "You will excuse me for having cluttered it up with my things; to-morrow I will take them away. You see I had not dared hope you would come back to me. I had expected to go to you."

"I and you--you and I." The girl repeated the words after her, slowly, as if trying to grasp their full meaning as she uttered them. Then a sudden terror leaped into her eyes, and she cried shudderingly: "Oh, how strange it is!"

"You do not doubt it? You do not doubt it still?" exclaimed Miss Ludington, in anguished tones.

"No, no!" said the girl, recovering herself with an evident effort. "I cannot doubt it. I do not," and she threw her aims about Miss Ludington's neck in an embrace in which, nevertheless, a subtle shrinking still mingled with the impulse of tenderness which had overcome it.

When presently Miss Ludington and Ida went upstairs together, the latter, with eager, unhesitating step, led the way through a complexity of roundabout passages, and past many other doors, to that of the chamber which had been the common possession of the girl and the woman. Miss Ludington followed her, wondering, yet not wondering.

"It seems so strange to see you so familiar with this house," she said, with a little hysterical laugh, "and yet, of course, I know it is not strange."

"No," replied the girl, looking at her with a certain astonishment, "I should think not. It would be strange, indeed, if I were not familiar here. The only strange thing is to feel that I am not at home here, that I am a guest in this house."

"You are not a guest," exclaimed Miss Ludington, hurriedly, for she saw the dazed look coming again into the girl's eyes. "You shall be mistress here. Paul and I ask nothing better than to be your servants."

To pass from the waking to the dreaming state is in general to exchange a prosaic and matter-of-fact world for one of fantastic improbabilities; but it is safe to assume that the three persons who fell asleep beneath Miss Ludington's roof that morning, just as the birds began to twitter, encountered in dreamland no experiences so strange as those which they had passed through with their eyes open the previous evening.

CHAPTER IX.

The day following, Paul was downstairs before either Ida or Miss Ludington. He was sitting on the piazza, which was connected with the sitting-room by low windows opening like doors, when he heard a scream, and Ellen, the housemaid, who had been busy in the sitting-room, ran out upon the piazza with a face like a sheet.

"What's the matter?" he demanded.

"Sure I saw a ghost!" gasped Ellen. "I was on a chair dusting the picture, as I always does mornings, an' I looked up, an' there in the door stood the very same girl that's in the picture, kind of smiling like. And so I give a yell an' run."

As she spoke Ida stepped out upon the piazza, and precipitately sheltering herself behind Paul, Ellen whispered, "Sure there she is now!"

On seeing that, instead of sharing her terror, he cordially greeted the ghost, the girl's face showed such comical bewilderment that Ida smiled and Paul laughed outright.

"This is no ghost, Ellen. This lady is Miss Ida Ludington, a relative of Miss Ludington's, who came to live here last night."

"I hope ye'll not mind me takin' ye for a ghost, miss," said Ellen, confusedly; "but sure ye are the livin' image of the picture, and me not knowin' anybody was in the house more than the family;" and she disappeared to tell her story in the kitchen.

Ida's appearance was noticeably calmer than the night before. There was, indeed, no indication of excitement in her manner. Paul inquired how she had slept.

"I should think you might have had strange dreams," he said.

"I did not dream at all. I slept soundly," she replied. "But this morning when I woke up and recognized the familiar features of the room I have always slept in-

-the same books, the same pictures, the furniture just as ever--I had to sit down a long time to collect my thoughts and remember what had happened. I could remember it well enough, but to realize it was very hard. And then, when I went to the window and looked out and saw the meeting-house and the school-house and the neighbours' houses, just where I have seen them from that window all my life since I was a baby, I had to sit down and think it all over, again before I could believe that I was not in Hilton, and last night all a dream."

She spoke in a low, even tone, which was so evidently the result of an effort at self-control, that it impressed Paul more than any display of mental perturbation would have done.

At this moment Miss Ludington appeared on the piazza with a white, excited face, which, however, as soon as she saw Ida, became all smiles.

She had scarcely slept at all. The thought had kept her awake that Ida might vanish as mysteriously as she had come, and be gone at morning. From sheer weariness, however, she had at last fallen into a doze. On awaking she had gone to call Ida, and finding her chamber empty, had hurried downstairs full of apprehension.

Immediately after breakfast, Miss Ludington, to whom Ellen's mistake, if mistake it could be called, had been related, took Ida upstairs, and made her exchange her white dress of the fashion of half a century before for one of her own, in order that her appearance might excite less remark among the servants pending the obtaining of a suitable wardrobe from the city.

There was another consideration which made the change of costume not only desirable, but necessary.

Ida's dress, which had not seemed the night before, to casual examination, to differ from other cloth, had begun to crumble away in a very curious manner. The texture seemed strangely brittle and strengthless. It fell apart at a touch, and was reduced to a fine powder under the pressure of the fingers. She could not possibly have worn it even one day.

The dress of Miss Ludington's, for which she exchanged it, had been made for that lady when considerably stouter than at present, but was with difficulty enlarged sufficiently for the full figure of the girl. Like all but the latest of Miss Ludington's dresses, it was of deepest black, and, strikingly beautiful as Ida had been in white, the funereal hue set off the delicacy of her complexion, the pure expression of her face, and the golden lustre of her hair, like fresh revelations.

Paul was left pretty much to himself during the day. A large part of it was spent by the ladies in an upstairs chamber, which Miss Ludington had devoted to a collection of mementoes of the successive periods of her life from infancy.

"Come," she had said to Ida, "I want to introduce you to the rest of the family. I want to make you acquainted with the other Miss Ludingtons who have borne the name between your time and mine."

Having been an only child, Miss Ludington's garments, toys, school-books, and other belongings had not been handed down to younger brothers and sisters, and eventually to destruction. It had been an easy matter to preserve them, and, consequently, the collection was large and curious, including samples of the wardrobe appertaining to every epoch, from the swaddling-clothes of the infant to a black gown of the last year.

After the period of youth, however, which Ida represented, the number and interest of the mementoes rapidly decreased, and for many years had consisted of nothing more than a few dresses and a collection of photographs, one or two for each year, arranged in order. They numbered not less than fifty in all and covered thirty-seven years, from a daguerreotype of Miss Ludington at the age of twenty-five to a photograph taken the last month. Between these two pictures there was not enough resemblance to suggest to a casual observer that they were pictures of the same individual.

To trace the gradual process of change from year to year during the intervening period, was an employment which never lost its pensive fascination for Miss Ludington. For each of these faces, with their so various expressions, represented a person possessing a peculiar identity and certain incommunicable qualities--a person a little different from any one of those who came before or after her, and from any other person who ever lived on earth.

As now the grey head and the golden head bent together over one picture after another, Miss Ludington related all she could remember of the history and personal peculiarities of the original.

"There is, really, not much to say about them," she said. "They lived very quiet, uneventful lives, and to anybody but us would, doubtless, seem entirely uninteresting persons. All wore black dresses, and had sad faces, and all found in their thoughts of you the source at once of their only consolation and their keenest sorrow. For they fully believed--think of it!--fully and unquestionably believed that you were dead; more hopelessly dead than if you were in your grave, dead, with no possibility of resurrection."

"This is the one," she said, presently, as she took up the picture of a woman of thirty-five, "who had the fortune left to her, which has come down to me. I want you to like her. Next to you I think more of her than I do of any of the rest. It was she who cut loose from the old life at Hilton which had become so sour and sad, and built this new Hilton here, where life has been so much calmer, and, on the whole, happier, than it had got to be at home. It was she who had the portrait of you painted which is downstairs."

Ida took up a picture of the Miss Ludington of twenty-six or seven.

"Tell me something about her," she said. "What kind of a person was she?"

The elder woman's manner, when she saw what picture it was that Ida had taken up, betrayed a marked embarrassment, and first she made no reply.

Noticing her confusion and hesitation, Ida said, softly, "Don't tell me if it is anything you don't like to speak of. I do not care to know it."

"I will tell you," replied Miss Ludington, with determination. "You have as good a right to know as I have. She cannot blame me for telling you. She knows your secrets as I do, and you have a right to know hers. She had a little escapade. You must not be too hard on her. It was the outcome of the desperate dulness and life-weariness that came over her with the knowledge that youth and its joys were past, leaving nothing in their place. The calm and resignation to a lonely existence, empty of all that human hearts desire, which came in after-years, she could not yet command. Oh, if you could imagine, as I remember, the bitterness of that period, you would not be too hard upon her for anything she might have done! But, really, it was nothing very bad. People would not call it so, even if it had ever become known." And then, with blushing cheeks and shamed eyes, Miss Ludington poured into Ida's ears a story that would have disappointed any one expectant of a highly sensational disclosure, but which stood out in her memory as the one indiscretion of an otherwise blameless life. That she imparted it to Ida was the most striking evidence she could have given of the absolute community of interests which she recognized as existing between them. She was greatly comforted when Ida, instead of appearing shocked, declared that she sympathized with the culprit more than she blamed her, and that her misconduct was venial.

"I suppose," said Miss Ludington, "every one, in looking back upon their past selves, sees some whom they condemn, and, perhaps, despise, and others whom they admire and sympathize with. And I confess I sympathize with this poor girl. Those I don't like are some whom I remember to have lacked softness of heart, to have been sour and ungenerous; these, for instance," indicating certain pictures. "But it is hardly fair," she added, laughing, "for us two to get together and abuse the rest of the family, who, no doubt, if they were present, would have something to say for themselves, and some criticisms to offer on us--that is, on me. None of them would criticize you. You were the darling and pride of us all."

"If I do say it," Miss Ludington presently resumed, "we have been a very respectable lot on the whole. The Ida Ludingtons have been good babies, good children, good girls, good women, and, I hope, will prove to have been respectable old women. In the spirit land, when we all meet together, there will be no black sheep among us, nor even anybody that we shall need to send to Coventry: But I do not see why special affinities should not assert themselves there as here, and cliques form among us. You will belong to them all, of course, but next to you I know that I shall be fondest of that poor girl I told you about, of her and of the Ida Ludington who built this new Hilton thirty years ago."

"And now," she said, as they finished looking over the pictures and talking about them, "I have introduced you to all who have borne our name from your day to mine. As to those who came before you, the baby Ida and the child Ida, you remember them even better than I do, no doubt. I would give anything if I had their pictures, but the blessed art of photography was not then invented. These keepsakes are all I have of them." And taking Ida over to another part of the room, she showed her a cradle, several battered dolls, fragments of a child's pewter tea-set, and a miscellaneous collection of toys.

They took up and handled tenderly pairs of little shoes, socks nearly as long as one's fingers, and baby dresses scarcely bigger than a man's mittens. Lying near were the shoes, and gowns, and hoods, now grown a little larger, of the child, with the coral necklace, and first precious ornaments, the dog's-eared spelling-books, and the rewards of merit, testifying of early school-days.

"I can barely remember the baby and this little girl," said Miss Ludington, "but I fancy they will be the pets of all the rest of us up there, don't you?"

After Miss Ludington had shown Ida all the contents of the room, and they were about to leave it, she said to the girl, "And now what do you think of us other Ida Ludingtons, who have followed you, present company not excepted? Confess that you think the acquaintances I have introduced to you were scarcely worth the making. You need not hesitate to say so; it is quite my own opinion. We have amounted to very little, taken altogether."

"Oh, no!" said Ida, quietly; "I do not think that; I would not say that; but your lives have all been so different from what I have always dreamed my life as a woman would be."

"You have a right to be disappointed in us," said Miss Ludington. "We have, indeed, not turned out as you expected--as you had a right to expect." But Ida would not admit in any derogatory sense that she was disappointed.

"You are sweeter, and kinder, and gentler, than I supposed I ever could be," she said; "but you see, I thought, of course, I should be married, and have children, and that all would be so different from what it has been; but not that I should ever be better than you are, or nearly so sweet. Oh, no!"

"Thank you, my darling!" said the old lady, kissing Ida's hand, as if she were a queen who had conferred an order of merit upon her. "I think that to have to confess to their youthful selves their failures to fulfil their expectations must be the hardest part of the Day of Judgment for old folks who have wasted their lives. All will not find so gentle a judge as mine."

Her eyes were full of happy tears.

In the latter part of the afternoon they took a walk in the village, and Ida pressed her companion with a multitude of inquiries about the members of the families which had occupied the houses, forty and fifty years before, and what had since become of them; to reply to which taxed Miss Ludington's memory not a little.

As they came to the schoolhouse Ida ran on ahead, and when her companion entered, was already seated in Miss Ludington's old seat. Nothing, perhaps, could have brought home to the latter more strongly the nature of her relationship to Ida than to stand beside her as she sat in that seat.

As they fell to talking of the scholars who had sat here and there, Miss Ludington began gently to banter Ida about this and that boyish sweetheart, and divers episodes connected with such topics.

"This is unfair," said the girl, smiling. "It is a very one-sided arrangement that you should remember all my secrets while I know none of yours. It is as if you had stolen my private journal."

A subtle coyness, an air of constraint, and of shy, curious observance, which had marked Ida's manner toward Miss Ludington in the early part of the day, had noticeably given way under the influence of the latter's blithe affectionateness, and it was with arms about each other's waists that the two sauntered back to the house, in the twilight.

"I scarcely know what to call you," said Ida. "For me to call you Ida, as you call me, would be and, besides, you are so much older than I it would seem hardly fitting."

Miss Ludington laughed softly.

"On the score of respect, my darling, you need not hesitate," she said, "for it is you who are the elder Miss Ludington, and I the younger, in spite of my white hair. You are forty years older than I. It is I who owe you the respect due to years. You are right, however; it would be confusing for us to call each other by the same name, and still there is no word in human language that truly describes our relationship."

"It seems to me it is more like that of sisters than any other," suggested Ida, with a certain timidity.

Miss Ludington reflected a moment, and then exclaimed, delightedly:

"Yes, we will call each other sister, for our relation is certainly a kind of sisterhood. We are, like sisters, not connected directly, but indirectly, though our relation to our common individuality, as if we were fruit borne by the same tree in different seasons. To be sure," she added regarding her blooming companion with a smile of tender admiration, "we can scarcely be said to look as much alike as sisters commonly do, but that is because there is not often a difference of more than forty years in the ages of sisters."

And so it was agreed that they should call each other sister.

Although it was but one day that these two had been known to each other, yet so naturally had Ida seemed drawn towards Miss Ludington, and so spontaneous had been the outflow of the latter's long-stored tenderness toward the girl, that they were already like persons who have been bosom friends and confidants for years.

In this wonderfully rapid growth of a close and tender intimacy, Miss Ludington exultingly recognized the heart's testimony to the reality of the mystic tie between them.

So fit and natural had the presence of Ida under her roof already come to seem, that she found herself half-forgetting, at times, the astounding and tragic circumstances to which it was due.

Absorbed in the wonder and happiness of her own experience, Miss Ludington had barely given a thought to Paul during the day. Having been constantly with Ida she had not, indeed, seen him, save at table, and had failed to take note of his wobegone appearance. At any other time it would have aroused her solicitude; but it was not strange that on this day she should have had no thought save for herself and her other self.

It had, indeed, been a day of strangely mingled emotions for Paul.

Supposing a lover were separated from his mistress, and that the privilege of being with her, and spending his days in sight of her, were offered him by some fairy, but only on condition that all memory of him should be blotted from her mind, and that she should see in him merely a stranger--is it probable, however great might be the desire of such a lover to behold his mistress, that he would consent to gratify it on these terms?

But it was with Paul as if he had done just this. That the sight of his idol should have fallen to his lot on earth; that he should hear the sound of her voice, and breathe the same air with her, was, on the one hand, a felicity so undreamed of, a fortune so amazing, that he sometimes wondered how he could enjoy it, and still retain his senses.

But when he met her, and she returned his impassioned look with a mere smile of civil recognition; when he spoke to her, and she answered him in a tone of conventional politeness--he found it more than he could bear.

The eyes of her picture were kinder than hers. He had, at least, been able to comfort himself with the belief that, as a spirit, she had known of his love, and accepted it. Now, by her incarnation, while his eyes had gained their desire, his heart had lost its consolation.

His condition of mind rapidly became desperate. He could not bear to be in Ida's presence. Her friendly, formal accent was unendurable to him. Their blank, unrecognizing expression, as they rested on him in mere kindliness, made her lovely eyes awful to him as a Gorgon's.

In the early evening he found Miss Ludington alone, and broke out to her:

"For God's sake, can't you help me? I shall go mad if you don't!"

"Why, what do you mean?" she exclaimed, in astonishment. "Don't you see?" he cried. "She does not know me. I have lost her instead of finding her. I, who have loved her ever since I was a baby, am no more than a stranger to her. Can't you see how she looks at me? She has learned to know you, but I am a stranger to her."

"But how could she know you, Paul? She did not know me till it was explained to her."

"I know," he said. "I don't blame her, but at the same time I cannot stand it. Can't you help me with her? Can't you tell her how I have loved her, so that she may understand that at least?"

"Poor Paul!" said Miss Ludington, soothingly. "In my own happiness I had almost forgotten you. But I can see how hard it must be for you. I will help you. I will tell her all the story. Oh, Paul! is she not beautiful? She will love you, I know she will love you when she hears it, and how happy you will be--happier than any man ever was! I will go to her now."

And, leaving Paul vaguely encouraged by her confidence, she went to find Ida.

She came upon her in the sitting-room, intently pondering the picture above the fireplace.

"I want to tell you a love story, my sister," she said.

"Whose love story?" asked Ida.

"Your own."

"But I never had a love story or a lover. Nobody can possibly know that better than you do."

"I will show you that you are mistaken," said Miss Ludington, smiling. "No one ever had so fond or faithful a lover as yours. Sit down and I will tell you your own love story, for the strangest thing of all is that you do not know it yet."

Beginning with Paul's baby fondness for her picture, she related to Ida the whole story of his love for her, which had grown with his growth, and, from a boyish sentiment, become the ruling passion of the man, blinding him to the charms of living women, and making him a monk for her sake.

She described the effect upon him of the first suggestion that it might be possible to communicate with her spirit, and how her presence on earth was due to the enthusiasm with which he had insisted upon making the attempt.

Then she asked Ida to imagine what must be the anguish of such a lover on finding that she did not know him--that he was nothing more than a stranger to her. She told her how, in his desperation, he had appealed to her to plead his case and to relate his story, that his mistress might at least know his love, though she might not be able to return it.

Ida had listened at first in sheer wonder, but as Miss Ludington went on describing this great love, which all unseen she had inspired, to find awaiting her full-grown on her return to earth, her cheek began to flush, a soft smile played about her lips, and her eyes were fixed in tender reverie.

"Tell him to come to me," she said, gently, as Miss Ludington finished.

When Paul entered, Ida was alone, standing in the centre of the room.

He threw himself at her feet, and lifted the hem of her dress to his lips.

"Paul, my lover," she said softly.

At this he seized her hand and covered it with kisses. She gently drew him to his feet. He heard her say, "Forgive me, Paul; I did not know."

Her warm breath mingled with his, and she kissed him on the lips.

CHAPTER X.

In the days that followed, Ida was the object of a devotion on the part of Miss Ludington and Paul which it would be inadequate to describe as anything less than sheer idolatry. Her experience was such as a goddess's might be who should descend from heaven and take up her abode in bodily form among her worshippers, accepting in person the devotion previously lavished on her effigy.

With Miss Ludington this devotion was the more intense as it was but a sublimed form of selfishness, like that of the mother's to her child, whom she feels to be a part, and the choicest part, of her own life. The instinct of maternity, never gratified in her by the possession of children, asserted itself toward this radiant girl, whose being was so much closer to hers than even a child's could be, whose life was so wonderfully her own and yet not her own, that, in loving her, self-love became transfigured and adorable. She could not have told whether the sense of their identity or their difference were the sweeter.

Her delight in the girl's loveliness was a transcendent blending of a woman's pleasure in her own beauty and a lover's admiration of it. She had transferred to Ida all sense of personal identity excepting just enough to taste the joy of loving, admiring, and serving her.

To wait upon her was her greatest happiness. There was no service so menial that she would not have been glad to perform it for her, and which she did not grudge the servants the privilege of rendering. The happiness which flooded her heart at this time was beyond description. It was not such a happiness as enabled her to imagine what that of heaven might be, but it was the happiness of heaven itself.

As might be expected, the semi-sacredness attaching to Ida, as a being something more than earthly in the circumstances of her advent, lent a rare strain to

Paul's passion.

There is nothing sweeter to a lover than to feel that his mistress is of a higher nature and a finer quality than himself. With many lovers, no doubt, this feeling is but the delusion of a fond fancy, having no basis in any real superiority on the part of the loved one. But the mystery surrounding Ida would have tinged the devotion of the most prosaic lover with an unusual sentiment of awe.

Paul compared himself with those fortunate youths of antiquity who were be-loved by the goddesses of Olympus, and in whose hearts religious adoration and the passion of love blended in one emotion.

Ever since that night when her heart had been melted by the story of his love, Ida had treated him with the graciousness which a maiden accords to an accepted lover. But far from claiming the privileges which he might apparently have enjoyed, it seemed to him presumption enough and happiness enough to kiss her dress, her sleeve, a tress of her hair, or, at most, her hand, and to dream of her lips.

The dazed appearance, as of one doubtful of herself and all about her, which Ida had worn the night when she was brought home, had now wholly passed away. But a certain pensiveness remained. Her smiles were the smiles of affection not of gaiety, and there was always a shadow in her eyes. It was as if the recollection of the mystery from which her life had emerged were never absent from her mind.

Still she took so much pleasure in her daily drives with Miss Ludington that the latter ordered a pony chaise for her special use, and when Paul arranged a croquet set on the village green, she permitted him to teach her the game, and even showed some interest in it.

When the first dresses which had been ordered for her came home, she was delighted as any girl must have been, for they were the richest and most beautiful fabrics that money could buy; but Miss Ludington seemed, of the two, far the more pleased.

For herself she had cared nothing for dress. In forty years she had not given a thought to personal adornment, but Ida's toilet became her most absorbing preoc-cupation. On her account she became a close student of the fashion-papers, and but for the girl's protests would have bought her a new dress at least every day.

She would have liked Ida to change her costume a dozen times between morn-ing and evening, and asked no better than to serve as her dressing-maid. To brush and braid her shining hair, stealthily kissing it the while; to array her in sheeny satins and airy muslins; to hang jewels upon her neck, and clasp bracelets upon her wrists, and to admire and caress the completed work of her hands, constituted an occupation which she would have liked to make perpetual.

When Miss Ludington's mother had died she had left to her daughter, then a young girl, all her jewels, including a rather flue set of diamonds. When one day Miss Ludington took the gems from the box in which they had been hidden away for half a lifetime, and hung them upon Ida, saying, "These are yours, my sister," the girl protested, albeit with scintillating eyes, against the greatness of the gift.

"Why, my darling, they are yours," replied Miss Ludington. "I am not making you a gift. It was to you that mother gave them. I only return you your own. When you left the world I inherited them from you, and now that you have come back I return them to you."

And so the girl was fain to keep them.

Thus it had come about that before Ida had been in the house a week it was no longer as a mystery, or, at least, as an awe-inspiring mystery, but as an ineffably dear and precious reality, that her presence was felt. Had a stranger chanced to come there on a visit, at that time, he would doubtless have been struck with the fact that a young girl was the central figure of the household, around whom its other members revolved; but it is probable that this fact, in itself not unparalleled in American households, would have seemed to such an observer sufficiently explained by the unusual gentleness and beauty of the girl herself. The necessity of a supernatural explanation certainly would not have occurred to him.

The servants had been merely informed that Ida was a relative of Miss Ludington's, and though they were very curious as to what connection she might be, their speculations did not extend beyond the commonly recognized modes of relationship. The housekeeper, indeed, who had been in Miss Ludington's employ many years, and supposed she knew all about the family, thought it strange that she could recall no young lady relative answering to Ida's description. But as she found that her most ingenious efforts entirely failed to extract any information on the subject from Miss Ludington, Paul, or Ida herself, she was obliged, like the rest, to accept the bare fact that the new-comer was Miss Ida Ludington, and that she was somehow related to Miss Ludington; a fact speedily supplemented by the discovery that to please Miss Ida was the surest way to the favour of Miss Ludington and Mr. Paul.

On that score, however, there was no need of any special inducement, Ida's sweet face, and gracious, considerate ways, having already made her a favourite with all who were attached to the household.

It was ten days or a fortnight after Ida had been in the house that Miss Ludington received a letter from Dr. Hull, in which that gentleman said that he should do himself the honour of calling on her the following day.

He said she might be interested to know that he had already received several communications from Mrs. Legrand, through mediums, in which she had declared herself well content to have died in demonstrating so great a truth as that immortality is not individual, but personal. She considered herself to be most fortunate in that her death had not been a barren one, as most deaths are; but that in dying, she had been permitted to become the second mother of another, and far brighter life than hers had been. She felt that she had made a grand barter for her own earthly existence, which had been so sick and weary.

The bulk of Dr. Hull's letter, which was quite a long one, consisted of further quotations from Mrs. Legrand's communications.

She said that she had been welcomed by a great multitude of spirits, who to her had owed the beginning of their recognition on earth, and that their joy over this discovery, which should bring consolation to many mournful mortals, as well as to themselves, was only equalled by their wonder that it had not been made years before. It appeared that, since intercourse between the two worlds had first begun, it had been the constant effort of the spirits to teach this truth to men; but the stupid refusal of the latter to comprehend had till now baffled every attempt. How it had been possible that men who had reached the point of believing in immortality at all should be content to rest in the inadequate and preposterous conception that it only attached to the latest phase of the individual, was the standing wonder of the spirit world.

It was as if one should throw away the contents of a cup of wine, and carefully preserve the dregs in the bottom.

That so loose an association of personalities as the individual, and those personalities so utterly diverse, no two of them even alive at the same time, should have impressed even the most casual observer as a unit of being--a single person--was accounted a marvel by the angels. If men had believed all the members of a family to have but one soul among them, their mistake would have been more excusable, for the members of a family are, at least, alive at the same time, while the persons of an individual are not even that.

Dr. Hull said that he had gathered from Mrs. Legrand's communications that she had seen many things which would teach mortals not to grieve for their departed friends, as for shades exiled to a world of strangers. To such mourners she sent word that their own past selves, who have likewise vanished from the earth, are keeping their dear dead company in heaven. And far more congenial company to them are these past selves than their present selves would be, who, through years and changes since their separation, have often grown out of sympathy with the departed, as they will find when they shall meet them. The aged husband, who has mourned all his life the bride taken from him in girlhood, will find himself well-nigh a stranger to her, and his mourning to have been superfluous; for all these years his own former self, the husband of her youth, has borne her company.

Dr. Hull said, in closing, that, as probably Miss Ludington would presume, his particular motive in making bold to break in upon her privacy was a desire, which he was sure she would not confound with vulgar curiosity, to see again the young lady who had succeeded to his friend's earthly life in so wonderful a manner, and to learn, what, if any, were the later developments in her case. He was preparing a book upon the subject, in which, of course without giving the true names, he intended to make the facts of the case known in the world. Its publication, he felt assured, would mark a new departure in spiritualism.

Miss Ludington read the letter aloud to Ida and Paul, as all three sat together in the gloaming on the piazza. As Paul from time to time, during the reading, glanced at Ida he noticed that she kept her face averted.

"I am glad," said Miss Ludington, as she finished the letter, "that Mrs. Legrand is happy. It is so hard to realize that about the dead. The feeling that, our happiness was purchased by her death has been the only cloud upon it. And yet it would be strange indeed if she were not happy. As she says, she did not die a barren death, but in giving birth. And it was no tiny infant's existence, of doubtful value, that she exchanged her life for, but a woman's in the fulness of her youth and beauty. Such a destiny as hers never fell to a mother before."

"Never before," echoed Paul, rising to his feet in an access of enthusiasm; "but who shall say that it may not often fall to the lot of women in the ages to come, as the relations between the worlds of men and of spirits, become more fully known? The dark and unknown path that Ida trod that night back to our world will, doubtless, in future times, become a beaten and lighted way. This woman through whom she lives again did not die of her own choice; but I do not find it incredible that many women will hereafter be found willing and eager to die as she did, to bring back to earth the good, the wise, the heroic, and beloved. The world will never need to lose its heroes then, for there will never lack ardent and devoted women to contend for such crowns of motherhood."

He stopped abruptly, for he had observed that Ida's face betrayed acute distress.

"Forgive me," he said. "You do not like us to talk of this."

"I think I do not," she replied, in a low voice, without looking up. "It affects me very strangely to think about it much. I would like to forget it if I could and feel that I am like other people."

She had, in fact, shown a marked and increasing indisposition almost from the first to discuss the events of that wonderful night at Mrs. Legrand's. After having had the circumstances once fully explained to her, she had never since referred to them of her own accord.

She apparently had the shrinking which any person, and especially a woman, would naturally have from the idea of being regarded as something abnormal and uncanny, and mingled with this was, perhaps, a certain sacred shamefacedness, at the thought that this most intimate and vital mystery of her second birth had been witnessed and was the subject of curious speculations.

CHAPTER XI.

The ladies were out driving, the following afternoon, when Dr. Hull arrived, but Paul was at home. He brought out some cigars, and they made themselves comfortable on the piazza.

Dr. Hull was full of questions about Ida? how she appeared; what relations had established themselves between Miss Ludington and her; whether she showed any memory whatever of her disembodied state; whether the knowledge of the mystery involving her seemed in any way to affect her spirits or temper, or to set her apart in her own estimation from others, with many other acute and carefully considered queries calculated to elicit the facts of her mental and spiritual condition?

"There is one point," said the doctor, "about which I am particularly curious. How is it with her memory of her former life on earth? Does it break off suddenly, as if on some particular day or hour her spirit had made way for its successor, and passed away from earth?"

"On the contrary," said Paul, "she has intimated, in talking over the past with Miss Ludington, that the memory of her life on earth is clear and precise during its earlier portions, but that toward the last it grows hazy and indistinct."

"Exactly," broke in the doctor. "Just as if her personality had a little overlapped and melted at the edge into that which followed it. Yes, it is as I thought it might be. Youth, or childhood, or infancy, or any other epoch of life, does not abruptly cease and give place to another. Their souls are gradually withdrawn as the light is withdrawn from the sky at evening, and a space of twilight renders the transition from one to the other perceptible only in the result, not in the process. This I think is a view of the matter, that is corroborated by the testimony of our own consciousness, don't you, Mr. De Riemer?"

"On the whole, yes," replied Paul. "And still, if she had said that the severing of her personality from that which succeeded it was sharp and clearly defined, so that up to a certain day, or even hour, her memory was full and distinct, and then became a blank, there are passages in my own experience, and I think in that of many persons, which her statement would have made comprehensible. I think that to many, perhaps to all persons of reflective turn of mind, there come days, even hours, when they feel that they have suddenly passed from one epoch of life into another. A voice says in their hearts with unmistakable clearness, 'Yesterday I was young; to day I am young no longer.' There is also sometimes a day, I think, when the middle-aged man becomes suddenly aware that he is old. Who shall deny the truth of these intuitions, or say that it is not in that very day and hour that the spirit of youth or of maturity takes its flight?"

"By the way," said Dr. Hull, "have you ever speculated on the probable number of the souls of an individual? It is an interesting question."

"I suppose that the number may greatly differ in different individuals," replied Paul. "In individuals of many-sided minds and versatile dispositions, there are, perhaps, more distinct personalities than constitute an individual of less complex character. But how many in either case only God can tell. Who can say? It may be that with every breath which I expire a soul or spiritual impression of myself is sent forth. The universe is large enough even for that. Such may at least be the case in moments of special intensity, when we live, as we say, a year in an hour."

They smoked on awhile in silence. Presently Paul said, "When the world comes to recognize the composite character of the individual, that it is composed of not one, but many persons, a new department will be added to ethics, relating to the duties of the successive selves of an individual to one another. It will be recognized, on the one hand, that it is the duty of a man to fulfil all reasonable obligations incurred by his past selves, on the same principle that a pious son fulfils the equitable obligations incurred by a parent. This duty is, indeed, recognized to-day, although not on the correct basis. As regards the ethical relation of a man to the selves who succeed him, a wholly new idea will be introduced. It will be seen that the duty of a man to lead a wise life, to be prudent, to make the most of his powers, to maintain a good name, is not a duty to himself, merely an enlightened selfishness, as it is now called, but a genuine form of altruism, a duty to others, as truly as if those others bore different names instead of succeeding to his name. It will be seen that a man's duty to his later selves is like the duty of a father to his helpless children: to provide for their inheritance, to see that he leaves them a sound body and a good name, if nothing more. It will be perceived that the man who is charitably called 'his own worst enemy,' is not only no better, but worse, than if he were the enemy of his neighbours, because he is blasting coming lives that have a far nearer claim upon him than any neighbour can have.

"There will arise, also, in that day, I fancy," said Paul, "some rather delicate questions, as to how far a man may properly bind his future selves by pledges and engagements which he has no means of knowing will meet with their approval, and which may quite possibly prove intolerable yokes to them."

"Ah!" exclaimed the doctor, "that is indeed an interesting point. And, meanwhile, I should say the intelligible discussion of these questions will involve a modification in grammatical usage. If we believe that our present selves are distinct persons from our past selves, it is manifestly improper to use the first person in speaking of our past selves. Either the third person must be used, or some new grammatical form invented."

"Yes," said Paul. "If entire accuracy is sought the first person cannot be properly employed by any one in referring either to his past or his future selves, to what has been done or to what will be done by them."

At this moment the carriage drew up before the house, and Paul helped the ladies out.

Miss Ludington greeted Dr. Hull cordially, and stopped upon the piazza in hat and shawl to talk with him. But Ida merely bowed stiffly, with lowered eyes, and passed within.

Before they were called to tea Paul found an opportunity to tell the doctor how sensitive Ida was to any discussion of the mystery connected with her, and to suggest that at table any direct reference to the subject should be avoided.

The expression of disappointment on Dr. Hull's countenance seemed to indicate that he had anticipated thoroughly cross-questioning her in the interest of spiritual science; but he said that he would regard Paul's suggestion, and even admitted that it was, perhaps, natural she should feel as she did, although he had not anticipated it.

At the table, therefore, Ida was spared any direct reference to herself as a phenomenon, and although Dr. Hull talked of nothing but spiritualism and the immortality of past selves, it was in their broad and general aspects that the subjects were discussed.

"Your nephew," he said to Miss Ludington, "has evidently given much time and profound thought to these matters; and although I am an old man, and have been more interested in the spiritual than the material universe for these many years, I was glad of an opportunity to sit at his feet this afternoon."

Turning to Paul, he added, "What you were saying about the possibility that souls, or, at least, spiritual impressions, destined to eternity, are given forth by us constantly, as if at every breath, is wonderfully borne out in a passage from a communication I had from Mrs. Legrand yesterday, to which I meant to have alluded at the time you were speaking. She said that those who supposed that the spirit-land contained only one soul for every individual that had ever lived had no conception of its vastness, and that the stream of souls constantly ascending is like a thick mist rising from all the earth. The phrase struck me as strangely strong, but I can conceive now how she might have come to use it.

"What is your conjecture, or have you none at all," he added, after a moment's thought, still addressing Paul, "as to the relation which will exist in the spirit-land among the several souls of the same individual?"

"It seems to me," said Paul, "that the souls of an individual, being contemporaneous over there, and all together in the eternal present, will be capable of blending in a unity which here on earth, where one is gone before another comes, is impossible. The result of such a blending would be a being which, in stead of shining with the single ray of a soul on earth, would blaze from a hundred facets simultaneously. The word 'individual,' as applied here on earth, is a misuse of language. It is absurd to call that an individual which every hour divides. The, earthly stage of human life is so small that there is room for but one of the persons of an individual upon it at one time. The past and future selves have to wait in the side scenes. But over there the stage is larger. There will be room for all at once. The idea of an individual, all whose personalities are contemporaneous, may there be realized, and such an individual would be, by any earthly measurement, a god.

"But there are many individuals," he pursued after a pause, "of which we cannot imagine a blending of the successive persons to be possible. There, for instance, are cases where there exist radical and bitter oppositions and differences of character, and propensity between the youth and the manhood of the individual. In the case of such ill-assorted personalities a divorce *ex vinculo individui* may be the only remedy; and, possibly, the parties to it may be sent back to earth, to take their chances of finding more congenial companions."

Ida had not said a word during the time they had sat at table. She had, indeed, scarcely lifted her eyes from her plate.

As they rose she challenged Paul to a game at croquet, for which the twilight left ample opportunity.

Miss Ludington and Dr. Hull sat upon the piazza in full view of the players.

"What do you call her?" he asked, abruptly, after a pause in their conversation.

"Why, we call her Ida, of course," replied Miss Ludington, with some surprise. "What else could we call her? Is not her name Ida Ludington?"

"On my own account," said Dr. Hull, "I should not have needed to ask you, because I am acquainted with the circumstances of the reassumption of her earthly life and name, but how would you introduce her to one who was not so acquainted--to any one, in fact, besides yourself, your nephew, and myself?"

"In the same way, I suppose," replied Miss Ludington.

"Precisely," said the doctor "but if they were acquainted with your family, or if they took any special interest in her, would they not want to know what was the nature of her relationship to you? She could not be your daughter. They would ask what was her connection with your family. To tell them the truth would be of no use at all, for no one on earth would believe what we know to be true, nor could I blame them, for I, myself, would not have believed it if I had not been a witness."

Miss Ludington was silent a while. Then she said: "It does not matter; we see few, I may say no strangers, or even acquaintances; we live alone. It is enough that we know her."

"Yes," replied the doctor. "It is, indeed, quite another thing to what it would be if you had a large circle of acquaintances. So long as you live, it is not important, and I presume that your health is good."

"What is it that is not important?" demanded Miss Ludington.

"Why that she should have a name," replied the doctor, lifting his eyebrows with an expression of slight surprise. "Unfortunately, the courts do not recognize such a relation as exists between you and this young lady. You are the only Miss Ludington in the eye of the law, and she is non-existent, or, at least, an anonymous person. She has not so much as a name sign on a hotel-register. But so long as you live to look after her she is not likely to suffer."

"But I may die!" exclaimed Miss Ludington.

"In that case it would be rather awkward for her," said the doctor. "She would die with you in the eye of the law" and here he branched off into rather a fantastical discourse on the oddities and quiddities of the law and lawyers, against whom he seemed to have a great grudge.

"But, Dr. Hull, what can I do about it?" said Miss Ludington, as he quieted down.

"Excuse me. About what?"

"How can I give her a name in the eye of the law?"

"Oh--ah--exactly? Well, that's easy enough; there are two ways. You can adopt her, or some young fellow can marry her, and if I were a young man--if you'll excuse an old gentleman for the remark--it would not be my fault if she were not provided with a legal title very soon."

Declining Miss Ludington's proposal to send him to the ferry in her carriage, the doctor, soon after, took his leave.

He paused as he passed the croquet-ground and stood watching the players. It came Ida's turn, and he waited to see her play. It was a very easy shot which she had to make; she missed it badly. He bade them good-evening, and went on.

CHAPTER XII.

It was but a few days after Dr. Hull's visit that Miss Ludington had a sudden illness, lasting several days, which, during its crisis, caused much alarm.

Ida turned all the servants out of the sick-room and constituted herself nurse, watcher, and chambermaid, if she lay down at all it was only after leaving a substitute charged to call her upon the slightest occasion. Light and quick of step, strong and gentle of hand, patient, tireless, and tender, she showed herself an angel of the sick-room.

There was, indeed, something almost eager in the manner in which she seized upon this opportunity of devoting herself to Miss Ludington, and the zeal with which she made the most of every possibility of rendering her a service. She seemed, in fact, almost sorry when the patient had no further need of her especial attendance.

To Miss Ludington the revelation that she was so dear to Ida was profoundly affecting. It was natural that she should adore Ida, but that Ida should be correspondingly devoted to her touched her in proportion to its unexpectedness. "I should be glad to be sick always, with you to nurse me, my sister," she said. Whenever she addressed Ida by this title of sister her voice lingered upon the syllables as if she were striving to realize all the mysterious closeness and tenderness of the relation between them which its use implied.

The period of convalescence, during which Miss Ludington sat in her room, lasted several days, and one evening she sent for Paul. She was alone when he came in, and after he had inquired after her condition, she motioned him to a chair.

"Sit down, Paul," she said; "I want to have a little talk with you."

He sat down and she went on: "I find that I have been greatly enfeebled by this attack, and though the doctor tells me I may regain reasonable health, he warns me that I shall not live for ever, and that when I die I may die without much warn-ing."

Expressions of mingled grief, surprise, and incredulity from Paul interrupted her at this point, but she presently went on:--

"It is really nothing to distress yourself over, my dear child. He does not say that I may not live on indefinitely, but only that when death comes he is likely to enter without knocking, and I'm sure any sensible person would much rather have it so. It was of Ida that I wanted to speak to you. Since I have been sick, and espe-cially since what the doctor told me, I have been thinking what would become of her if I should die. Did you ever consider, Paul, that she has not even a name? The world does not recognize the way by which she came back into it, and in the eye of the law she has no right to the name of Ida Ludington, or to any other."

"I suppose not," said Paul.

"It does not matter while I live," pursued Miss Ludington; "but what if I should die?"

"Let us not talk of that," replied Paul, "or think of it. Yet even in that event I should be here to protect her."

Miss Ludington regarded the young man for some moments without speaking, and then, as a slight colour tinged her cheek she said, "Paul, do you love her?"

"Do you need to ask me that?" he answered.

"No, I do not," she replied; and then as she cast down her eyes, and the colour in her cheek grew deeper, she went on: "You know, Paul, that, as society is consti-tuted, there is but one way in which a young man can protect a young girl who is not his relative, and that is by marrying her. Have you thought of that?"

Paul's face flushed a deep crimson, and his forehead reddened to the roots of the hair; after which the colour receded, and he became quite pale; and then he flushed again deeper than before, till his eyes became congested, and he saw Miss Ludington sitting there before him, with downcast eyes and a spot of colour in ei-ther cheek, as through a fiery mist.

Yes, he had thought of it.

The idea that, being of mystery though she was, Ida was still a woman, and that he might one day possess her as other men possess their wives, had come to him, but it had caused such an ungovernable ferment in his blood, and savoured withal of such temerity, that he had been fairly afraid to indulge it. In the horizon of his mind it had hovered as a dream of unimaginable felicity which might some day in the far future come to pass; but that was all.

Finally he said, in a husky voice, "I love her."

"I know you do," replied Miss Ludington. "No one but myself knows how you have loved her. You are the only man in the world worthy of her, but you are worthy even of her."

"But she would not marry me," said Paul. "She is very good to me, but she has never thought of such a thing. It is I that love her, and she is very good to let me; but she does not love me. How should she?"

"I think she does," said Miss Ludington, with a tone of quiet assurance. "I have never said anything to her about it; but I have observed her. A woman can generally read a woman in that particular, and it would be especially strange if I could not read her. I do not think that you need to be afraid of her answer. I shall not urge her by a word; but if she is willing to be your wife, it will be by far the best way her future could be provided for. Then, however soon I might die, she would not miss me."

Paul had heard distinctly only her first words, in which she had stated her belief that Ida loved him and would probably be his wife. This intimation had set up such a turmoil in his brain that he had not been able to follow what she had subsequently said. There was a roaring in his ears. Her voice seemed to come from very far away, nor did he remember how long afterwards it was that he left her.

As he went downstairs the door of the sitting-room stood open, and he looked in. Ida sat there reading.

The weather was very warm, and her dress was some gauzy stuff of a pale-green tint which set off her yellow hair and bare arms and throat with sumptuous effect. She was a ravishing symphony in white, pale green, and gold.

She had not heard his approach, and was unconscious of his gaze. As he thought of her as the woman who might be his wife, he grew so faint with love, so intimidated with a sense of his presumption in hoping to possess this glorious creature, that, not daring to enter, he fled out into the darkness to compose himself.

No experience of miscellaneous flirtations, or more or less innocent dalliance, had ever weakened the witchery of woman's charms to him, or dulled the keenness of his sensibility to the heaven she can bestow. For an hour he wandered about the dark and silent village street, waiting for the tumult of his emotions to subside sufficiently to leave him in some degree master of himself. When at last he returned to the house, his nerves strung with the resolution to put his fortune to the test, Ida was still in the sitting-room where he had left her.

Miss Ludington's conversation with Paul had left her in a mood scarcely less agitated than his. The sensation with which she had watched his devotion to Ida during the past weeks had been a sort of double-consciousness as if it were herself whom Paul was wooing, although at the same time she was a spectator. The thoughts and emotions which she ascribed to Ida agitated her almost as if they had been experienced in her proper person.

It was a fancy of hers that between herself and Ida there existed a species of clairvoyance, which enabled her to know what was passing in the latter's mind--a completeness of rapport never realized between any other two minds, but nothing more than might be expected to attend such a relationship as theirs, being a foretaste of the tie that joins the several souls of an individual in heaven. She had never had a serious love affair in her life, but now, in her old age, she was passing through a genuine experience of the tender passion through her sympathetic identification with Ida.

As she sat in her chamber after Paul had gone, fancying herself in Ida's place, imagining what she would hear him say, what would be her feelings, and what she would answer, her cheeks flushed, her breath came quickly, and there was a dew like that of dreaming girlhood in her faded eyes.

She was still flushing and trembling when there came a soft knock on her door, and Paul and Ida stood before her.

Ida was blushing deeply, with downcast face, and the long lashes hid her eyes. She stood slightly bending forward, her long beautifully moulded arms hanging straight down before her. She looked like a beautiful captive, and Paul, as he clasped her waist with his arm, and held one of her hands in his, looked the proudest of conquerors.

"I did not know but I might be dreaming it," he said, "and so I brought her for you to see. She says she will be my wife"

CHAPTER XIII.

Paul's courtship of Ida really began the night when he took her in his arms as his promised wife, for although she had called him her lover before, his devotion, while impassioned enough, had been too distant and wholly reverential to be called a wooing. But the night of their betrothal his love had caught from her lips a fire that was of earth, and it was no longer as a semi-spiritual being that he worshipped her, but as a woman whom it was no sacrilege to kiss a thousand times a day, not upon her hand, her sleeve, or the hem of her dress, but full upon the soft warm mouth.

This transformation of the devotee into the lover on his part was attended by a corresponding change in Ida's manner toward him. A model relieved from a strained pose could not show more evident relief than she did in stepping down from the pedestal of a tutelary saint, where he had placed her, to be loved and caressed like an ordinary woman, for if the love had at first been all on his side, it certainly was not now.

"I'm so glad," she said one day, "that you have done with worshipping me. Think of your humbling yourself before me, you who are a hundred thousand times better, and wiser, and greater than I. Oh, Paul it is I who ought to worship you, and who am not good enough to kiss you," and before he could prevent her she had caught his hand, and, bowing her face over it, had kissed it. As he drew it away he felt that there were tears upon it. It was evening, and he could not see her face distinctly.

"Darling," he exclaimed, "what is the trouble?"

"Oh, nothing at all!" she replied. "It is because I am in love, I suppose."

Whether it was because she was in love or not it is certain that she took to crying very often during these days. Her manner with her lover, too, was often strangely moody. Sometimes she would display a gaiety that was almost feverish, and shortly after, perhaps, he would surprise her in tears. But she always declared that she was not unhappy; and, unable to conceive of any reason why she should be, Paul was fain to conceive that she was merely nervous.

The absorption of the lovers in each other's society naturally left Miss Ludington more often alone than before; but Ida was very far from neglecting her for her lover. Her care for her since her sickness was such as a daughter might give to a beloved and invalid mother. It was an attention such as the lonely old lady had never enjoyed in her life, or looked for, and would have been most grateful to have had from any one, but how much more from Ida!

The village street was a rarely romantic promenade on moonlight evenings, and the twanging of Paul's guitar was often heard till after midnight from the meeting-house steps, which were a favourite resort with the lovers. Those steps, in the Hilton of Miss Ludington's girlhood, had been a very popular locality with sentimental couples, and she well remembered certain short-lived romances of Ida's first life on earth with which they had been associated. One night, when the young people had lingered there later than usual, Miss Ludington put on her shawl and stepped across the green to warn them that it was time for even lovers to be abed.

As she approached, Paul was seated on the lower step, touching his guitar, and facing Ida, who sat on the step above leaning back against a pillar. A blotch of moonlight fell upon her dreamy, upturned face. One hand lay in her lap, and the fingers of the other were idly playing with a tress of hair that had fallen over her bosom. How well Miss Ludington remembered that attitude, and even the habit of playing with her hair which Ida had in the days so long gone by.

She stood in the shadow watching her till Paul ceased playing. Then she advanced and spoke to them.

"I have been standing here looking at you, my sister," she said. "I have been trying to imagine how strangely it must come over you that forty years ago you sat here as you sit here now, just as young and beautiful then as now, and Paul not then born, even his parents children at that time."

Ida bent down her head and replied, in scarcely audible tones, "I do not like to think of those days."

"And I don't like to think of them," echoed Paul, with a curious sensation of jealousy, not the first of the kind that he had experienced in imagining the former life of his darling. "I do not like to think who may have sat at her feet then. I, too, would like to forget these days."

Ida bent her head still lower and said nothing. It was Miss Ludington who spoke.

"You have no ground to feel so," she said. "I can bear her witness--and what better witness could you have?--that till now she never knew what it is to love. It is true she sat here then as now, and there were others at her feet, drawn by the same beauty that has drawn you, but their voices never touched her heart. She had to come back again to earth to learn what love is."

Paul bent contritely, and kissed Ida's feet as she sat above him, murmuring, "Forgive me!" Her hand sought his and pressed it with convulsive strength.

They walked home in silence, gentle Miss Ludington inwardly reproaching herself for the embarrassment her words had seemed to cause Ida. She examined her memory afresh. It was very long ago; she was growing old, and it was natural to suppose that her memory might be losing in distinctness. Perhaps some, of the sweethearts of that far away time had been a little nearer, a little dearer, to Ida than to her own fading memory they seemed to have been. Perhaps she had done a stupid thing in referring to those days.

Meanwhile, despite of circumstances that would seem peculiarly favourable to a young girl's happiness, Ida's tendency to melancholy was increasing upon her at a rate which began to cause Miss Ludington as well as Paul serious anxiety. She had indeed been pensive from the first, but the expression of her face, when in repose, had of late become one of profound dejection. The shadow which they had never been able to banish from her eyes had deepened into a look of habitual sadness. Coming upon her unexpectedly, both Miss Ludington and Paul had several times found her in tears, which she would not or could not explain. Not infrequently, when she was alone with her lover, and they had been silent awhile, he had looked up to find her eyes fixed upon him and brimming with tears, and at other times, when he was in the very act of caressing her, she would burst out crying, and sob in his arms.

But her unaccountable reluctance to consent to any definite arrangement for her marriage with the man she tenderly loved, and had promised to wed, was the most marked symptom of something hysterical in her condition.

Some three weeks had elapsed since she had given her word to be Paul's wife, but though he had repeatedly begged her to name a day for their wedding, he had entirely failed to obtain any satisfactory reply. When he grew importunate, the only effect was to set her to crying, as if her heart would break. He was completely perplexed. If she did not love him her conduct would be readily explainable; but that she was in love with him, and very much in love with him, he had increasing evidence every day.

She gave nothing that could be called a reason for refusing to say when she would marry him, though she talked feebly of its being so soon, and of not being ready; but when he reminded her of the special considerations that made delay inexpedient, of her own peculiarly unprotected condition, and of Miss Ludington's uncertain health, and desire to see them married as soon as possible, she attempted no reply, but took refuge in tears, leaving him no choice but to relinquish the question, and devote himself to soothing her.

When, finally, Miss Ludington asked Paul what were their plans, and he told her of Ida's strange behaviour, they took troubled counsel together concerning her.

It was evident that she was in a state of high nervous tension, and her conduct must be attributed to that. Nor was it strange that the experiences through which she had passed in the last month or two, supplemented by the agitations of so extraordinary a love affair, should have left her in a condition of abnormal excitability.

"She must not be hurried," said Miss Ludington. "She has promised to be your wife, and you know that she loves you; that ought to be enough to give you patience to wait. Why, Paul, you loved her all your life up to the last month without even seeing her, and did not think the time long."

"You forget," he replied, "that it is seeing her which makes it so hard to wait."

A day or two later, when she chanced to be sitting alone with her in the afternoon, Miss Ludington said: "When are you and Paul to be married?"

"It is not decided yet," Ida replied, falteringly.

"Has not Paul spoken to you about it?"

"Oh, yes!"

"I had hoped that you would have been married before this," said Miss Ludington, after a pause. "You know why I am so anxious that there should be no delay in assuring your position. The time is short I know, but the reasons against postponement are strong, and if you love him I cannot see why you should hesitate. Perhaps you are not quite sure that you do love him. A girl ought to be sure of that."

"Oh, I am quite sure of that! I love him with all my heart," exclaimed Ida, and began to cry.

Miss Ludington sat down beside her, and, drawing the girl's head to her shoulder, tried to soothe her; but her gentleness only made Ida sob more vehemently.

Presently the elder lady said, "You are nervous, my little sister, don't cry, now. We won't talk about it any more. I did not intend to say a word to urge you against your wishes, but only to find out what they were. You shall wait as long as you please before marrying him, and he shall not tease you. Meanwhile I will see to it that, if I should die, you will be left secure and well provided for, even if you never marry any one."

"What do you mean?" asked Ida, raising her head and manifesting a sudden interest.

"I will adopt you as my daughter," said Miss Ludington, cheerily. "Won't it be odd, pretending that you are my daughter, and that instead of coming into the world before me you came in after me? But it is the only way by which I can give you a legal title to the name of Ida Ludington, although it is yours already by a claim prior to mine. I would rather see you Paul's wife, and under his protection, but this arrangement will secure your safety. You see, until you have a legal name I cannot make you my heir, or even leave you a dollar."

"Do you mean that you want to make me your heir?" exclaimed Ida.

"Of course," said Miss Ludington. "What else could I think of doing? Even if you had married Paul, do you suppose I would have wished to have you dependent on him? I should then have left you a fortune under the name of Mrs. De Riemer. As it is, I shall leave it to my adopted daughter, Ida Ludington. That is the only difference."

"But, Paul?"

"Don't fret about Paul," replied Miss Ludington. "I shall not neglect him. I have a great deal of money, and am able to provide abundantly for you both."

"Oh, do not do this thing! I beg you will not," cried Ida, seizing Miss Ludington's hands, and looking into her face with an almost frenzied expression of appeal. "I do not want your money. Don't give it to me. I can't bear to have you. You have given me so much, and you are so good to me!--and that I should rob Paul, too! Oh, no I you must not do it; I will never let you."

"But, my darling," said Miss Ludington, soothingly, "think what you are to me, and what I am to you. Of course you cannot be conscious of our relation, in the absolute way I am; through the memory I have of you. I can only prove what I am to you by argument and evidence, but surely I have fully proved it, and you must not let yourself doubt it; that would be most cruel. To whom should I leave my money if not to you? Are we not nearer kin than two persons ever were on earth before? What have been the claims of all other heirs since property was inherited compared with yours? Have I not inherited from you all I am--my very personality--and should not you be my heir?

"And remember," she went on, "it is not only as my heir that you have a claim on me; your claim would be almost as great if you were neither near nor dear to me. It was through my action that you were called back, without any will of your own, to resume the life which you had once finished on earth. I did not intend or anticipate that result, to be sure, but I am not the less responsible for it and being thus responsible, though you had been a stranger to me instead of my other self, I should be under the most solemn obligation to guard and protect the life I had imposed on you."

While Miss Ludington was speaking Ida's tears had ceased to flow, and she had become quite calm. She seemed to have been impressed by what Miss Ludington had said. At least she offered no further opposition to the plan proposed.

"I am very anxious to lose no time," said Miss Ludington, presently, "and I think we had better drive into Brooklyn the first thing to-morrow morning, and see my lawyer about the necessary legal proceedings."

"Just as you please," said Ida, and presently, pleading a nervous headache, she went to her room and remained there the rest of the afternoon.

Meanwhile Paul had seen Miss Ludington, and she had told him of her talk with Ida, and its result. The young man was beside himself with chagrin, humiliation, and baffled love. The fact that Ida had consented to the plan of adoption showed beyond doubt that she had given up all idea of being his wife, at least for the present, and possibly of ever marrying him at all.

Why had she dealt with him so strangely? Why had she used him with such cruel caprice? Was ever a man treated so perversely by a woman who loved him? Miss Ludington could only shake her head as he poured out his complaints to her. Ida's contradictory behaviour was as much a puzzle to her as to him, and she deplored it scarcely less. But she insisted that he should not trouble the girl by demanding explanations of her, as that, by vexing her, would only make matters worse.

If, indeed, Paul had any disposition to take the attitude of an aggrieved person, it vanished when he met Ida at the tea-table. The sight of her swollen eyes and red lids, and the piteous looks, of deprecating tenderness which from time to time she bent on him, left room for nothing in his heart but a great love and compassion. Whatever might be the secret of this strange caprice it was evidently no mere piece of wantonness. She was suffering from it as much as he.

He tried to get a chance to talk with her; but Miss Ludington, feeling slightly ill, went to her room directly after tea, and Ida accompanied her to see that she was properly cared for, and got comfortably to bed. After waiting a long while for her to come downstairs, Paul concluded that she did not intend to appear again, and went off for a walk, in the hope thereby of regaining something of his equanimity.

It was about ten o'clock when he returned home. As he came in sight of the house he saw by the light reflected from the sitting-room windows that there was some one upon the piazza. As he came nearer he perceived that it was Ida. She was sitting sidewise upon a long, cane-bottomed settee, and her arms were thrown upon the back of it to form a sort of pillow on which her head rested. His tread upon the turf was inaudible, and she neither saw nor heard him as he approached, nor when, softly mounting the steps, he stood over her.

She was indeed sobbing with such violence that she could not have been easily sensible of anything external. Paul had never heard such piteous weeping. He had never seen much of women's crying, and he did not know what abandonment of grief their tender frames can sustain--grief that seemingly would kill a man if he could feel it. Long, gurgling sobs followed one another as the waves of the sea sweep over the head of a straggling swimmer. Every now and then they were interrupted by sharp cries of exquisite anguish, such as might be wrung out by the sudden twist of a rack, and then would come a low, shrill crooning sound, almost musical, beyond which it seemed grief could not go.

The violence of the paroxysm would pass, and she would grow calmer, drawing long, shuddering breaths as she struggled back to self-control. Then a quick panting would begin and grow faster and faster, till another burst of sobs shook her like a leaf in the storm.

In very awe of such great grief Paul stood awhile silently over her, the tears filling his own eyes and running down his cheeks unheeded. She had wept something like this, though nothing like so long or so bitterly, on former occasions, when he had urged her with special vehemence to fix a day when she would fulfil her promise to be his wife.

Now, as he pondered the piteous spectacle before him, the thought came over him that his first reverential instinct concerning her, that despite her resumption of a mortal form she was something more than mortal, was true, and that he had done wrong in so far forgetting it as to urge her to be his wife as if she were merely a woman like others. She herself did not know it, but surely this exceeding cruel crying was nothing else but the conflict between the love of the woman which went out to her earthly lover, and would fain make him happy, and the nature of the inhabitant of heaven, where there is neither marrying nor giving in marriage. This was the key to her inexplicable sorrow during the past weeks. This explained why, though she loved him so tenderly, the thought of becoming his wife was so intolerable to her.

So be it. Her nature could not sink to his, but his should rise to hers. This brief dream of earthly passion must pass. Better a thousand times that he should be disappointed in all that is dear to the heart of a man, than that he should grieve her thus. In that moment it did not seem hard to him to sacrifice the hopes of the man to the devotion of the lover. By one great effort he rose again to the level of the ascetic passion that had glorified his life up to these last delirious weeks. She had brought heaven to earth for him, but it should still be heaven, since her happiness demanded it.

And having reasoned thus, at last, for there seemed no end of her weeping, or any diminution of its bitterness, he touched her. She started, and turned her streaming eyes to him, then, seeing who it was, threw her arms around his neck, and, as he sat beside her, laid her head on his shoulder clinging to him convulsively.

"You don't believe I love you, Paul; and I can't blame you for it, I can't blame you," she sobbed; "but I do, oh, I do!"

"I do believe it. I know it," he said. "Don't think that I doubt it, and don't cry now, for after this your love shall be enough for me. I will not trouble you any more with importunings to be my wife. I have been very cruel to you."

"It is because I love you that I will not marry you," she sobbed. "Promise me you will never doubt that. Don't ask me to explain to you why it is; only believe me."

"I think I understand why it is already," he replied, gently. "I was very dull not to know before. If I had known, I should not have caused you so much grief."

She raised her head from his shoulder.

"What is it that you know?" she asked, quickly.

He thereupon proceeded to tell her, in tenderest words of reverence, what, in his opinion, was the mystical cause, unsuspected, perhaps, even by herself, of her unconquerable repugnance to the idea of being his wife, truly as he knew she loved him. He blamed himself that he had not recognized the sacred instinct which had held her back, but in his selfish blindness had gone on urging her to do violence to her nature. Now that his eyes were opened he would not grieve her any more. Her love alone should satisfy and bless him. Earthly passion should no more vex her serenity.

When he first began to speak she had regarded him with evident astonishment. As the meaning of his words became clear to her she had turned her face away from him and covered it with both her hands, as a person does under an overpowering sense of shame. She did not remove them until he had finished, when she rose abruptly.

Light enough came from the windows behind them for him to see that her cheeks and forehead were crimson.

"I think I may as well go now," she said. "Good-bye." And in another moment he found himself alone, not a little astonished at the suddenness of her departure.

CHAPTER XIV.

Ida passed with a quick step through the sitting-room and upstairs to her bed-room, where she locked the door and threw herself upon the bed in a paroxysm of tearless sobbing.

"I believe I have no more tears left," she whispered, as at last she raised herself and arranged her dishevelled hair.

She sat awhile in woful reverie upon the edge of the bed, and then crossed the room to a beautiful writing-desk which Miss Ludington had given her. She opened it, and, taking out several sheets of paper, prepared to write. "If I had not run upstairs that moment," she murmured, "I must have told him the whole horrible story. But it is better this way. I believe it would have killed me to see the look on his face. Oh, my darling, my darling! what will you think of me when you know?" and then she sat down to write.

She stopped so many times to cry over it that it was midnight when the writing was finished. It was a letter, and the superscription read as follows:--

"To my lover, Paul, who will never love me any mere after he reads this, but whom I shall love for ever:--

"This letter will explain to you why my room is empty this morning. I could stand it no longer: to be loved and almost worshipped, by those whom I was bascly deceiving. And so I have fled. You will never see me or hear from me again, and you will never want to after you have read this letter. All the jewellery and dresses, and everything that Miss Ludington has given me, I have left behind, except the clothes I had to have to go away in, and these I will return as soon as I get where I am going. Oh, my poor Paul! I am no more Ida Ludington than you are. How could you ever believe such a thing? But let me tell my shameful story in order. Perhaps it was not so strange that you were deceived. I think any one might have been who held the belief you did at the outset.

"I am Ida Slater, Mrs. Slater's daughter, whom she named after Miss Ludington, because she thought her name so pretty when they went to school together as children in Hilton. I was born in Hilton twenty-three years ago, several years after Miss Ludington left the village. My father is Mr. Slater, of course, but he is the person you know as Dr. Hull, which is an assumed name. Mrs. Legrand, who is no more dead than you are, is a sister of my father. Her husband is dead, and father acts as her manager, and mother helps about the seances, and does what she can in any way to bring a little money. We have always been very poor, and it has been very, very hard for us to get a living. Father is a man of education, and had tried many things before we came to this, but nothing succeeded. We grew poorer and poorer, and when this business came in our way he had to take up with it or send us to the almshouse. It is not an honest business, at least as we conducted it; but, oh, Paul! none of you that are rich understand that to a very poor man the duty of supporting his family seems sometimes as if it were the only duty in the world.

"Well, when mother came to visit Miss Ludington, and saw that picture which is so much like me, and so little, mother says, like what Miss Ludington ever was, and when she found out about your belief in the immortality of past selves, the idea first came to her of deceiving you.

"That story of mother's going to Cincinnati was a lie, to prevent your suspecting that she had anything to do with the business. Mrs. Rhinehart is an imaginary person. At first, the idea was only to get you interested in the seances, for the profit of the fees; but when they saw how entirely deceived you were by my resemblance to the picture, the scheme of getting me into this house occurred to them.

"Or rather it did not occur to them at all. It was you, Paul, yourself, who suggested it, when you said that night after the first seance, that if a medium died in a trance, you believed the materialized spirit could not dematerialize but would return to earth. But for that the idea would never have occurred to them.

"It seemed a daring plot, but many things favoured it. I had lived in Hilton up to within a few years, and knew every stick and stone of the old as well as the new part of the village. I had wandered all over the old Ludington homestead time and again. Mother knew as much about Miss Ludington's early life as she did herself, and could post me on the subject, and there was my wonderful resemblance to the picture, which, of itself, would be almost enough to carry me through.

"It was for my sake entirely that they proposed this scheme. My father and mother may be looked down upon by the world as a very poor kind of people, but they have always been very good to me. I will not have you blame them except as you blame me with them. They thought that in this way I could be rescued from the hard and questionable life which they were living, and in which they did not wish me to grow up. If the plan succeeded, and you were deceived and took me here, thinking me the true Ida, they believed that I would be secured a life of happiness and luxury. They had seen, too, how you were in love with the true Ida, and made no question that you would love me and marry me.

"It was that more than all, Paul, that decided me to do it. I had fallen in love with you that night of the first seance when I stood before you and you looked at me with such boundless, adoring love. I think it would have turned almost any girl's head to be looked at in that way. And then, Paul, you are very handsome.

"I always had a taste for acting. They used to say I would have done well on the stage, and the idea of playing a role so fine and so bold as this took my fancy from the start. It was that, Paul, that, and the notion of your making love to me, more than any thought of the wealth and luxury I might get a share in, which made me consent to the plan.

"That sickness of Mrs. Legrand's between the seances--I am telling you all, Paul--was only a sham, so that we might see how much in earnest you were, and to get time for me to learn by heart all mother could teach me about the Hilton of forty years ago and Miss Ludington's girlhood. There were so many lists of names to be kept in mind, and school-room incidents, picnics, and flirtations; but it was as interesting as a romance, and being a Hilton girl, it did not take me long to make myself as much at home with the last generation as with my own. Sometimes mother would say to me, 'Ida, if I did not know that you are a good girl, and would be good to Miss Ludington, I would not betray my old friend this way. I would not do it for any one but you, and if I did not believe that in deceiving her you would make her very happy--far happier than now.'

"I think, in spite of all, she was very fond of Miss Ludington, for she made me promise, again and again, that I would be very good to her, as if I could have helped being good to such a gentle, tender-hearted person as she.

"You see, in our business, we had shown to so many sad people what they believed to be the forms and faces of their dead friends, and had sent them away comforted, that we had come to feel our frauds condoned by the happiness they caused, and that we were, after all, doing good.

"As for you, Paul, mother had no scruples. She said that I was a good girl, and any man was lucky to get me. I was not sure of that, but I knew that any girl would be fortunate whom you loved. She had a dress cut for me in the exact pattern of that in the picture--a very old-fashioned pattern, but very becoming to me--and all was ready. You know the rest.

"I forgot to say that the reason the dress all fell to pieces the day after I came here was that it had been treated with a chemical preparation, which had completely rotted the texture of the cloth. Indeed I had trouble to keep it together that first night. Father saw to this part. He understands chemistry, and indeed, everything else except how to make a living.

"There was no trap-door in the floor in Tenth Street, but the whole ceiling of the cabinet was a trap-door, the edges hidden by the breadth of the boards forming the partition which enclosed it. It rose on oiled hinges, with a pulley and a counterweight, at a touch of a finger, and the person who was to appear, unless it was a part that the medium herself could take, descended in an instant by letting down a short light ladder, wrapped in cloth, so as to make no sound. The draught of air just before the appearance, which Miss Ludington had spoken of in her talks with me, was something that we never thought of, and was caused, I suppose, by the drawing of the air up through the raised ceiling.

"It was all so easy, so easy; we need not have taken half the precautions we did; you were so absolutely convinced from the first moment that I was the Ida of the picture. From the time I came home with you that night till now there has been no question of my proving who I was, but only of Miss Ludington's proving, and of your proving, to me, that you were the persons you claimed to be. It was not whether I was related to her, but only that she was related to me, which Miss Ludington thought in any need of demonstration.

"And as for you, Paul, it is not your fault that I was not your wife weeks ago.

"And so I should have been, and Miss Ludington's heir besides, but for two particulars in which our plot was fatally defective. It provided for all contingencies, but made no allowance for the possibilities that I might prove capable of gratitude towards Miss Ludington, and that I might fall in love with you. Both these things have happened to me, and there is no choice left me but to fly in the night. Of course I had expected you to fall in love with me, and had fancied you so much, after seeing you the first time, as to feel that it would be very fine to have you for a lover, and even for a husband. But that was not really love at all. I think if you could understand even a little what dismay came over me when I first realized that my heart was yours, you would almost pity me. After that, to deceive you was torture to me, and yet, to tell you the truth would have been to make you loathe me like a snake. Oh, Paul! think of what I have suffered these past weeks, and pity me a little!

"You will understand now why it was that I could not bear to have the circumstances of the fraud we had practised on you alluded to in my presence, and why, after the first few days, I never spoke of them myself.

"When father, whom you know as Dr. Hull, came that day to see how the plot was succeeding, I thought I should die with shame. He tried to catch my eye, and to get a chance to speak with me, but I avoided him. He must have gone away very much puzzled by my conduct, for it had been arranged between us that he should come. By that time, you see, I had become heart-sick of the part I was playing.

"But, Paul, you must not think that it was mere sham, father's drawing you out so much to talk at the table that night, and pretending to be so much taken up with what you said. He is great for being taken up with new ideas, and I think his interest was quite genuine. I knew before I left home that he half believed you to be right about the immortality of past selves. For my part, I believe it wholly, and that I have abused not only Miss Ludington and you, but the spirit of her whom I have personated.

"If Miss Ludington had not so loaded me with kindness I could have borne it, better, but to have that sweet old lady fairly worshipping the ground one trod on, and covering one with gifts, and dresses, and jewels, would have been too much, I think, for the conscience of the worst person in the world.

"I should have fled from the house before I had been here a week but for you, Paul. I could not bear to leave you. If I had only gone then I should have saved myself much; for what would it have been to leave you then to what it is now!

"It was very wrong in me to promise to marry you that night when you came to me; for I knew then as well as now that I never could. But I loved you so, I had no strength. Oh, these last happy weeks! I wonder if you have been so happy as I--so happy or so miserable, I don't know which to say; for all the time there was a deadly sickness at my heart, and every night I cried myself to sleep, and woke up crying; and yet I loved you so I could not but be happy in being where you were. Remember always, Paul, that if I had not loved you so, I should have let you marry an adventuress; for that is what I suppose you will call me now--you, who could not find words tender enough for me. Yes, if I had loved you less, I would have been your wife, and I would have made you very happy, just as we made so many poor people happy at our seances--by deceiving them. But I could not deceive you.

"It is true that I have been meanwhile deceiving you, but it has only been from day to day. I knew it was not to last, and I lacked strength to end it sooner. Think how dear your kisses must have been to me, that I could endure them with the knowledge all the while that if you knew whom you were kissing, you would spurn me with your foot.

"As soon as you began to urge me to name a day for our marriage I knew that the end was near. You wondered why I cried so whenever you spoke of it. You know now. To-day Miss Ludington told me that she intended to adopt me and leave me her fortune, so that I need feel under no necessity to marry you if I did not wish to. Think of that, Paul! Can you conceive of any one so low, so base, as to be capable of taking advantage of such a heart? As she was talking to me, I made up my mind that I must go to-night.

"This evening, when I was helping her to bed (I have been so glad to do all I could for her; it took away a little of my shame to see how happy I made her) she seemed so troubled because I could not keep my tears from falling. When you read her this she will think her sympathy wasted. And yet she will not think hard of me. She could not think hard of any one, and I am sure I love her dearly, and always shall.

"Oh, Paul, my darling, do not despise me utterly! My love was pure; it was as pure as any one's could be, though I have been so bad. I think my heart was breaking when you found me crying on the piazza to-night. It was not only that I must leave you, and never look on your face again, but that I must give over my memory to your scorn and loathing. When you took me in your arms and comforted me, my resolution all gave way, and I felt that I would not, could not, go. I think I was on the point of throwing myself at your feet and confessing all, and begging to be taken as the lowest servant in the house, so that I might be near you.

"And then it was that you began to explain to me that, although I might not be aware of it, the reason that I would not be your wife was that, having come from heaven, my nature was purer than that of earthly women, and shrank from marriage as a sacrilege.

"Think of your saying that to me!

"When I comprehended you, and saw that you actually believed what you said, I realized the folly of imagining that you could ever pardon me for what I had done, or that the gulf between what I was and what you thought me to be could ever be bridged. So it was that you yourself gave me back the resolution and the strength to leave you, which went from me when I was in your arms. I was overcome with such shame and self-contempt that I could not even kiss you as I left you for ever.

"I have told you my whole story, Paul, that you may know not alone how black my deception was, but how bitterly I have expiated it. I came into this house a frivolous girl; I leave it a broken-hearted woman. Do not blame me too harshly. It is myself that I have injured most. I leave you as well off as before you saw me; free to return to your spirit-love. She will forgive you. It is my only consolation that she is but a spirit-love. If she were a woman I could never have given you up to her. Never! Oh, Paul! If I could only hope that you would not wholly despise me, that you, would think sometimes a little pitifully of

"IDA SLATER."

She next wrote a note to Miss Ludington, full of contrition and tenderness, and referring her to Paul's letter for the whole story. It was after two o'clock in the morning when she finished the second letter, and laid it in plain view beside the other. She next removed her jewels and exchanged her rich costume for the simplest in her wardrobe, and having donned cloak and hat, extinguished the light, and softly unlocking the door, stepped into the hall.

Perfect silence reigned in the house. As she stood listening the clock in the sitting-room struck three. There was no time to lose. The early summer dawn would soon arrive, and, before the first servants of neighbours were stirring she must be outside the grounds and well on her way.

There was a late risen moon, and enough light penetrated the house to enable her to make her way without difficulty. As she passed Paul's door she stopped and stood leaning her forehead against the casement for some minutes. At last she knelt and pressed her lips to the threshold, and, choking down a sob, went on downstairs. As she passed through the sitting-room she paused a moment before the picture. "Forgive me," she whispered, looking up at the dimly visible face of Ida Ludington, and passed on. Unfastening a window that opened upon the piazza, she stepped forth and closed it behind her.

At the first light sound of her feet upon the walk, the mastiff that guarded the house bounded up to her, and seeing who it was, licked her hand. The big beast had fallen in love with her on her first arrival, and been her devoted attendant ever since. She sat down on the edge of the walk and put her arms around his neck, wetting his shaggy coat with her tears. Here was a friend who would know no difference between Ida Slater and Ida Ludington. Here was one who loved her for herself.

Presently she rose, dried her eyes, and went on down the street, the dog trotting contentedly behind her. As she came to a point beyond which the trees cut off the view of the house, she stood still, gazing back at it for a long time. Finally, with a gesture of renunciation, she turned and passed swiftly out of sight.

CHAPTER XV.

It was Miss Ludington herself who, stirring unusually early, discovered Ida's flight on going to her room.

Paul opened his eyes a few minutes later to see her standing by his bedside, the picture of consternation.

"She is gone!" she exclaimed.

"Who is gone?" he asked, rubbing his eyes.

"Ida has gone. Her room is empty."

Hastily dressing, he rejoined her in Ida's chamber, and together they went over the letters she had left.

If the revelation which they contained had been made when she had been in the house a shorter time, its effect might have been very different. But it had come too late to produce the revulsion of feeling it might then have caused. True, it was under a false name that she had first won their confidence, but it was the girl herself they had learned to love. If her name proved to be Ida Slater, why it was Ida Slater whom they loved. It was the person, not the name.

"Oh, why did she leave us!" cried Miss Ludington, with streaming eyes, as she finished Ida's letter to Paul. "Why did she not come to us and tell us! We would have forgiven her. She was not so much to blame as her parents. How can we blame her when we think how happy she has made us! Oh, Paul! we must find her. We must bring her back."

He pressed her hand in silence. His darling, his heart's love, had gone away from him, out into the world, and he knew not where to find her, and yet it would be hard to say whether there was not more of exultation than of despair in the mingled emotions which just then deprived him of the power of speech.

He had comprehended perfectly well her confession of the deception which she had practised on them, but the portion of her letter which had chiefly affected him had been the impassioned avowal of her love for him. After his recent trying ordeal in striving to subject an earthly love to spiritual conditions, culminating the night before in the renunciation of the hope of ever marrying her at all, there was an intoxicating happiness in the discovery that she was every whit as earthly as he, and loved him with a passion as ardent as his own. He was a Pygmalion, whose statue had become a woman. For the first time he now realized how far his heart had travelled from the spirit-love which once had been enough for it, and how impossible it was that it should ever again find satisfaction in the dim and nebulous emotion in which it had so long rested. With a sense of recreancy that was wholly shameless, he realized that it was no longer Ida Ludington, but Ida Slater, whom he loved.

Little did the forlorn girl, in her self-imposed exile, imagine what a welcome would have met her if, moved by some intuition, she had retraced her steps that morning to the chamber which a few hours before she had deserted.

Repentance often is so fine that in the moral balance it quite outweighs the fault repented of, and so it was in her case. Such repentance is as if the black stalk of sin had blossomed and put forth a fragrant flower.

These two persons, whom she had expected to loathe her as soon as they should know the truth, had from the first reading of her story been more impressed with the chivalrous instinct which had driven her to abandon her role of fraud when it was about to be crowned with dazzling success, than with her original offence in entering upon it. The effect of her story was in this respect a curious one for a confession to produce: it had added to the affection which they had previously entertained for her, an appreciation of the nobility of her character which they had not then possessed.

Paul's heart yearned after its mistress in her self-humiliation and voluntary banishment as never before. This impassioned and most human woman, who had shown herself capable of wrong, and, also, of most generous renunciation, had struck a deeper chord in his breast than had ever vibrated to the touch of the flawless seraph he had supposed her to be.

Having canvassed all possible methods of reaching Ida in her flight, it was decided by Paul and his aunt to begin by advertising, and that same day the following notice was inserted in all the daily papers of Brooklyn and New York;--

"IDA S----R.--All is forgiven; only come back. We cannot live without you. For pity's sake at least write to us.

"Miss L---- AND PAUL."

This advertisement was to remain in the papers till forbidden. If Ida was anywhere in the two cities or vicinity, the chances were that it would fall under the notice of herself or some of her family. Before inserting the advertisement Paul had visited Mrs. Legrand's house in East Tenth Street; but, as he had expected, he found that the family had moved away long previously, probably with a view to avoid detection, and to enable Mrs. Legrand to obtain business elsewhere.

A week passed without any response to the advertisement. Paul spent his days walking the streets of New York and Brooklyn at random, for the sake of the chance, about one in ten billions, that he might meet Ida. Anything was more endurable than sitting at home waiting, and by dint of tramping all day long he was so dead tired when he reached home at night that he could sleep, which otherwise would have been out of the question.

About the middle of the week a bundle arrived, containing the dress Ida had worn away, with her hat and cloak, but without a word of writing; Paul devoured them with kisses. A study of the express markings showed that the package must have been sent from Brooklyn, which went to show that Ida was in that city. Believing that she did not intend to respond to the advertisement, Paul had determined, if he did not hear from her within a few days, to employ a prominent New York detective firm to search for her. If he could but once see her face to face, he was sure that he could bring her back.

A week from the day on which she had fled he was starting out as usual, early in the morning, for another day of hopeless, weary tramping in the city, when the postman handed him a letter addressed in her handwriting. It was to him like a voice from the grave, and read as follows:--

"I have seen your advertisement for me. I cannot believe that you have forgiven me. You could not do it. It is impossible. Even if I could believe it, I do not think I should ever have the courage to face you after what you know of me. I should die of shame. Oh, Paul! if you could see how my cheeks burn as I write this, and know that you will see it. But I cannot deny myself the happiness of writing to you. There is no reason why we should not write sometimes, is there? though we never see each other. Does Miss Ludington really forgive me, or does she merely consent to have me return because you still care for me? If you do still care for me--Oh, Paul! I cannot believe it--do you forget what I have done? Read over again the letter I left for you when I came away. You must have forgotten it. Read it carefully. Think it all over. Oh, no, you cannot love me still!

"IDA SLATER."

Paul replied with the first love-letter he had ever written, and one that any woman who loved him must have found irresistible. He enclosed a note from Miss Ludington, assuring Ida of the unhappiness which her flight had caused them, the undiminished tenderness which they cherished for her; and the cruelty she would be guilty of if she refused to return.

In response to these letters there came a note saying simply, "I will come."

On the evening of the day this note was received, as Paul and Miss Ludington were together in the sitting-room talking as usual of Ida, and wondering on what day she would return, there was a light step at, the open door, and she glided into the room, and, throwing herself on her knees before Miss Ludington, hid her face in her lap.

It was an hour before she would raise her head, replying the while only with sobs to the kisses and caresses showered upon her, and the assurances of love and welcome poured into her ears.

When at last she lifted her face her embarrassment was so distressing that in pity Miss Ludington told Paul he might take her out for a walk in the dark.

When they came back her cheeks were flushed as redly as when she went out; but, despite her shame, she looked very happy.

"She is to be my wife in two weeks from to-day," said Paul, exultantly.

"I ought not to let him marry me. I know I ought not. I am not fit for him," faltered Ida; "but I cannot refuse him anything, and I love him so!"

"You are quite fit for him," said Miss Ludington, kissing her, "and I can well believe he loves you. It would be strange, indeed, if he did not. You are a noble and a tender woman, and he will be very happy."

In the days that followed, Ida was at first much puzzled to account not only for the evident genuineness of the esteem which her friends cherished for her, but for the fact that it seemed to have been enhanced rather than diminished by the recent events. Instead of regarding her repentance as at most offsetting her offence, they apparently looked upon it as a positive virtue redounding wholly to her credit. It was quite as if she had made amends for another person a sin, in contrast with whose conduct her own nobility stood out in fine relief.

And that, in fact, is exactly the way they did look at it. Their habit of distinguishing between the successive phases of an individual life as distinct persons, made it impossible for them to take any other view of the matter.

In their eyes the past was good or bad for itself, and the present good or bad for itself, and an evil past could no more shadow a virtuous present than a virtuous present could retroact to brighten or redeem an ugly past. It is the soul that repents which is ennobled by repentance. The soul that did the deed repented of is past forgiving. There was no affectation on the part of Paul or Miss Ludington of ignoring the fraud which Ida had practised, or pretending to forget it. This was not necessary out of any consideration for her feelings, for they did not hold that it was she who was guilty of that fraud, but another person.

As gradually she comprehended the way in which they looked upon her, and came to perceive that they unquestioningly held that she had no responsibility for her past self, but was a new being, she was filled with a great exhilaration, the precise like of which was, perhaps, never before known to a repentant wrong-doer. As they believed, so would she believe. With a great joy she put the shameful past behind her and took up her new life. "As a man thinketh in his heart so is he."

If she had loved Paul before, if she had before felt tenderly toward Miss Ludington, a passion of gratitude now intensified her love, her tenderness, a thousand-fold.

Miss Ludington's failing health was the only shadow on the perfect happiness of the lovers during those two weeks of courtship. Compared with the intoxicating reality of these golden days Paul looked back on his wooing of the supposed Ida Ludington as a vague and unsatisfying dream.

Now that Ida was no longer playing a part, he was really just becoming acquainted with her, and finding out what manner of maiden it was to whom he had lost his heart. Each day, almost each hour, discovered to him some new trait, some unsuspected grace of mind or heart, till, in this glowing girl, so bright, so blithe, so piquant, he had difficulty in recognizing any likeness, save of face and form, to the moody, freakish, melancholy, hysterical, and altogether eerie Ida Ludington.

"I am so glad," Miss Ludington said to her one day, "that you are Ida Slater, and not my Ida."

"Why are you glad?" Ida asked. "Would you not have been happier if you had gone on believing me to be your girlish self?"

"I should have grown very sad by this time if I had continued to think that you were she?" replied Miss Ludington. "I have not long to live, and it is far more important to me that she should be there to welcome me when I go over than that I should have her here with me for a few days before I go. If she were here on earth the thought of so soon leaving her behind would sadden me as much as the hope of meeting her now gladdens me."

Miss Ludington neither talked herself nor permitted others to talk in a melancholy tone of the probable nearness of her end. "Death may seem dreadful," she said to Ida one day, "to the foolish people who fancy that an individual dies but once, forgetting that their present selves are but the last of many selves already dead. The death which may now be near me is no sadder, no more important, than the deaths of my past selves, and no different, save in the single respect that this time no later self will follow me. This house of our individuality, which has sheltered us in turn, having become incapable of being repaired for the use of subsequent tenants, is to be pulled down. That is all."

Another time she said, "It is very strange to see people who dread death always looking for it instead of backward. In their fear of dying once they quite forget that they have died already many times. It is the most foolish of all things to imagine that by prolonging the career of the individual, death is kept at bay. The present self must die in any case by the inevitable process of time, whether the body be kept in repair for later selves or not. The death of the body is but the end of the daily dying that makes up earthly life."

They were married in the sitting-room before the picture that had exerted so strong an influence upon their lives. The servants were invited in, but there was no company. Ida wore a white satin with a low corsage, and as she stood directly below the picture, the resemblance impressed the beholders very strikingly. It was as if the girl had stepped down from the picture to be married.

Ida had demurred a little to standing just there, which had been the suggestion of Miss Ludington. She was not without a vague superstition that the spirit of the girl whose lover she had stolen away would not wish her well. But when she hinted this, Miss Ludington replied, "You must not think of it that way. What has a spirit like her to do with earthly passions? Your love has saved Paul from a dream as vain as it was beautiful, and which, had it gone on, might have gained a morbid strength and blighted his life. I like to fancy, and I know it is Paul's belief, that the spirit of my Ida influenced you to come to us just as you came, that under her form Paul might fall in love with you. In no other way but just this do I believe he could have been cured of his infatuation."

Owing to the precarious condition of Miss Ludington's health, Paul and Ida would not consent to leave home for any bridal trip.

It was but a week after the wedding that, on going into Miss Ludington's room as usual the first thing in the morning, Ida found her dead. She must have expired very quietly, if not, indeed, in her sleep, for her room adjoined that of the bridal couple, and she could have summoned Ida with the touch of a bell. Her features were relaxed in a smile of joyous recognition.

*   *   *   *   *   *

Paul took his wife to Europe directly after the funeral. One night, during their absence, a fire, probably set by tramps, broke out in one of the empty houses of the village, and, the wind being high and no help near, all the buildings on the place, including the homestead, were completely destroyed. The latter being shut up, nothing even of the furniture could be saved, and the entire contents, including the picture in the sitting-room, were consumed. The tourists were much shocked by the receipt of the intelligence, but Paul expressed the inmost conviction of both when he finally said, "Now that she is gone, perhaps it is as well. Ashes to ashes! The past has claimed its own."

They never rebuilt the village or the homestead, but on their return to this country took up their residence in New York. The site of the mimic Hilton is once more tilled as a farm.

It is scarcely necessary to add that Ida made such provision for her family as enabled them to retire from the medium business. Paul insisted that this provision should be at the most generous nature, for was he not indebted to them for the happiness of his life? He never would admit that Mrs. Legrand was a fraud, but always maintained that none but a truly great medium could have materialized the vaguest of love-dreams into the sweetest of wives.

As for Dr. Hull, or, rather, Mr. Slater, he became in time quite a crony of Paul's, and the book on which the latter is engaged, setting forth the argument for the immortality of past selves, will owe not a little to the suggestions of the old gentleman.

The Codes Of Hammurabi And Moses
W. W. Davies

QTY

The discovery of the Hammurabi Code is one of the greatest achievements of archaeology, and is of paramount interest, not only to the student of the Bible, but also to all those interested in ancient history...

Religion   **ISBN:** *1-59462-338-4*   **Pages:132**
MSRP $12.95

The Theory of Moral Sentiments
Adam Smith

QTY

This work from 1749. contains original theories of conscience amd moral judgment and It Is the foundation for systemof morals.

Philosophy **ISBN:** *1-59462-777-0*   **Pages:536**
MSRP $19.95

Jessica's First Prayer
Hesba Stretton

QTY

In a screened and secluded corner of one of the many railway-bridges which span the streets of London there could be seen a few years ago, from five o'clock every morning until half past eight, a tidily set-out coffee-stall, consisting of a trestle and board, upon which stood two large tin cans, with a small fire of charcoal burning under each so as to keep the coffee boiling during the early hours of the morning when the work-people were thronging into the city on their way to their daily toil...

Childrens   **ISBN:** *1-59462-373-2*

Pages:84
MSRP $9.95

My Life and Work
Henry Ford

QTY

Henry Ford revolutionized the world with his implementation of mass production for the Model T automobile. Gain valuable business insight into his life and work with his own auto-biography... "We have only started on our development of our country we have not as yet, with all our talk of wonderful progress, done more than scratch the surface. The progress has been wonderful enough but..."

Biographies/   **ISBN:** *1-59462-198-5*

Pages:300
MSRP $21.95

The Art of Cross-Examination
Francis Wellman

QTY

I presume it is the experience of every author, after his first book is published upon an important subject, to be almost overwhelmed with a wealth of ideas and illustrations which could readily have been included in his book, and which to his own mind, at least, seem to make a second edition inevitable. Such certainly was the case with me; and when the first edition had reached its sixth impression in five months, I rejoiced to learn that it seemed to my publishers that the book had met with a sufficiently favorable reception to justify a second and considerably enlarged edition. ...

Reference   ISBN: *1-59462-647-2*

Pages:412

MSRP $19.95

On the Duty of Civil Disobedience
Henry David Thoreau

QTY

Thoreau wrote his famous essay, On the Duty of Civil Disobedience, as a protest against an unjust but popular war and the immoral but popular institution of slave-owning. He did more than write—he declined to pay his taxes, and was hauled off to gaol in consequence. Who can say how much this refusal of his hastened the end of the war and of slavery ?

Law   ISBN: *1-59462-747-9*

Pages:48

MSRP $7.45

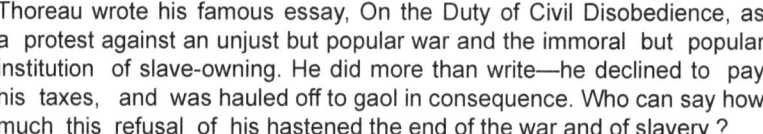

Dream Psychology Psychoanalysis for Beginners
Sigmund Freud

QTY

Sigmund Freud, born Sigismund Schlomo Freud (May 6, 1856 - September 23, 1939), was a Jewish-Austrian neurologist and psychiatrist who co-founded the psychoanalytic school of psychology. Freud is best known for his theories of the unconscious mind, especially involving the mechanism of repression; his redefinition of sexual desire as mobile and directed towards a wide variety of objects; and his therapeutic techniques, especially his understanding of transference in the therapeutic relationship and the presumed value of dreams as sources of insight into unconscious desires.

Psychology   ISBN: *1-59462-905-6*

Pages:196

MSRP $15.45

The Miracle of Right Thought
Orison Swett Marden

QTY

Believe with all of your heart that you will do what you were made to do. When the mind has once formed the habit of holding cheerful, happy, prosperous pictures, it will not be easy to form the opposite habit. It does not matter how improbable or how far away this realization may see, or how dark the prospects may be, if we visualize them as best we can, as vividly as possible, hold tenaciously to them and vigorously struggle to attain them, they will gradually become actualized, realized in the life. But a desire, a longing without endeavor, a yearning abandoned or held indifferently will vanish without realization.

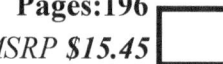

Self Help   ISBN: *1-59462-644-8*

Pages:360

MSRP $25.45

QTY

The Rosicrucian Cosmo-Conception Mystic Christianity *by Max Heindel* ISBN: 1-59462-188-8 **$38.95**
The Rosicrucian Cosmo-conception is not dogmatic, neither does it appeal to any other authority than the reason of the student. It is: not controversial, but is: sent forth in the, hope that it may help to clear... New Age/Religion Pages 646

Abandonment To Divine Providence *by Jean-Pierre de Caussade* ISBN: 1-59462-228-0 **$25.95**
"The Rev. Jean Pierre de Caussade was one of the most remarkable spiritual writers of the Society of Jesus in France in the 18th Century. His death took place at Toulouse in 1751. His works have gone through many editions and have been republished... Inspirational/Religion Pages 400

Mental Chemistry *by Charles Haanel* ISBN: 1-59462-192-6 **$23.95**
Mental Chemistry allows the change of material conditions by combining and appropriately utilizing the power of the mind. Much like applied chemistry creates something new and unique out of careful combinations of chemicals the mastery of mental chemistry... New Age Pages 354

The Letters of Robert Browning and Elizabeth Barret Barrett 1845-1846 vol II ISBN: 1-59462-193-4 **$35.95**
by Robert Browning and Elizabeth Barrett Biographies Pages 596

Gleanings In Genesis (volume I) *by Arthur W. Pink* ISBN: 1-59462-130-6 **$27.45**
Appropriately has Genesis been termed "the seed plot of the Bible" for in it we have, in germ form, almost all of the great doctrines which are afterwards fully developed in the books of Scripture which follow... Religion/Inspirational Pages 420

The Master Key *by L. W. de Laurence* ISBN: 1-59462-001-6 **$30.95**
In no branch of human knowledge has there been a more lively increase of the spirit of research during the past few years than in the study of Psychology, Concentration and Mental Discipline. The requests for authentic lessons in Thought Control, Mental Discipline and... New Age/Business Pages 422

The Lesser Key Of Solomon Goetia *by L. W. de Laurence* ISBN: 1-59462-092-X **$9.95**
This translation of the first book of the "Lernegton" which is now for the first time made accessible to students of Talismanic Magic was done, after careful collation and edition, from numerous Ancient Manuscripts in Hebrew, Latin, and French... New Age/Occult Pages 92

Rubaiyat Of Omar Khayyam *by Edward Fitzgerald* ISBN: 1-59462-332-5 **$13.95**
Edward Fitzgerald, whom the world has already learned, in spite of his own efforts to remain within the shadow of anonymity, to look upon as one of the rarest poets of the century, was born at Bredfield, in Suffolk, on the 31st of March, 1809. He was the third son of John Purcell... Music Pages 172

Ancient Law *by Henry Maine* ISBN: 1-59462-128-4 **$29.95**
The chief object of the following pages is to indicate some of the earliest ideas of mankind, as they are reflected in Ancient Law, and to point out the relation of those ideas to modern thought. Religion/History Pages 452

Far-Away Stories *by William J. Locke* ISBN: 1-59462-129-2 **$19.45**
"Good wine needs no bush, but a collection of mixed vintages does. And this book is just such a collection. Some of the stories I do not want to remain buried for ever in the museum files of dead magazine-numbers an author's not unpardonable vanity..." Fiction Pages 272

Life of David Crockett *by David Crockett* ISBN: 1-59462-250-7 **$27.45**
"Colonel David Crockett was one of the most remarkable men of the times in which he lived. Born in humble life, but gifted with a strong will, an indomitable courage, and unremitting perseverance... Biographies/New Age Pages 424

Lip-Reading *by Edward Nitchie* ISBN: 1-59462-206-X **$25.95**
Edward B. Nitchie, founder of the New York School for the Hard of Hearing, now the Nitchie School of Lip-Reading, Inc, wrote "LIP-READING Principles and Practice". The development and perfecting of this meritorious work on lip-reading was an undertaking... How-to Pages 400

A Handbook of Suggestive Therapeutics, Applied Hypnotism, Psychic Science ISBN: 1-59462-214-0 **$24.95**
by Henry Munro Health/New Age/Health/Self-help Pages 376

A Doll's House: and Two Other Plays *by Henrik Ibsen* ISBN: 1-59462-112-8 **$19.95**
Henrik Ibsen created this classic when in revolutionary 1848 Rome. Introducing some striking concepts in playwriting for the realist genre, this play has been studied the world over. Fiction/Classics/Plays 308

The Light of Asia *by sir Edwin Arnold* ISBN: 1-59462-204-3 **$13.95**
In this poetic masterpiece, Edwin Arnold describes the life and teachings of Buddha. The man who was to become known as Buddha to the world was born as Prince Gautama of India but he rejected the worldly riches and abandoned the reigns of power when... Religion/History/Biographies Pages 170

The Complete Works of Guy de Maupassant *by Guy de Maupassant* ISBN: 1-59462-157-8 **$16.95**
"For days and days, nights and nights, I had dreamed of that first kiss which was to consecrate our engagement, and I knew not on what spot I should put my lips..." Fiction/Classics Pages 240

The Art of Cross-Examination *by Francis L. Wellman* ISBN: 1-59462-309-0 **$26.95**
Written by a renowned trial lawyer, Wellman imparts his experience and uses case studies to explain how to use psychology to extract desired information through questioning. How-to/Science/Reference Pages 408

Answered or Unanswered? *by Louisa Vaughan* ISBN: 1-59462-248-5 **$10.95**
Miracles of Faith in China Religion Pages 112

The Edinburgh Lectures on Mental Science (1909) *by Thomas* ISBN: 1-59462-008-3 **$11.95**
This book contains the substance of a course of lectures recently given by the writer in the Queen Street Hail, Edinburgh. Its purpose is to indicate the Natural Principles governing the relation between Mental Action and Material Conditions... New Age/Psychology Pages 148

Ayesha *by H. Rider Haggard* ISBN: 1-59462-301-5 **$24.95**
Verily and indeed it is the unexpected that happens! Probably if there was one person upon the earth from whom the Editor of this, and of a certain previous history, did not expect to hear again... Classics Pages 380

Ayala's Angel *by Anthony Trollope* ISBN: 1-59462-352-X **$29.95**
The two girls were both pretty, but Lucy who was twenty-one who supposed to be simple and comparatively unattractive, whereas Ayala was credited, as her Bombwhat romantic name might show, with poetic charm and a taste for romance. Ayala when her father died was nineteen... Fiction Pages 484

The American Commonwealth *by James Bryce* ISBN: 1-59462-286-8 **$34.45**
An interpretation of American democratic political theory. It examines political mechanics and society from the perspective of Scotsman James Bryce Politics Pages 572

Stories of the Pilgrims *by Margaret P. Pumphrey* ISBN: 1-59462-116-0 **$17.95**
This book explores pilgrims religious oppression in England as well as their escape to Holland and eventual crossing to America on the Mayflower, and their early days in New England... History Pages 268

QTY

The Fasting Cure *by Sinclair Upton*   ISBN: *1-59462-222-1* **$13.95**
*In the Cosmopolitan Magazine for May, 1910, and in the Contemporary Review (London) for April, 1910, I published an article dealing with my experi-
ences in fasting. I have written a great many magazine articles, but never one which attracted so much attention... New Age/Self Help/Health Pages 164*

☐

Hebrew Astrology *by Sepharial*   ISBN: *1-59462-308-2* **$13.45**
*In these days of advanced thinking it is a matter of common observation that we have left many of the old landmarks behind and that we are now pressing
forward to greater heights and to a wider horizon than that which represented the mind-content of our progenitors...   Astrology Pages 144*

☐

Thought Vibration or The Law of Attraction in the Thought World   ISBN: *1-59462-127-6* **$12.95**

by William Walker Atkinson   *Psychology/Religion Pages 144*

☐

Optimism *by Helen Keller*   ISBN: *1-59462-108-X* **$15.95**
*Helen Keller was blind, deaf, and mute since 19 months old, yet famously learned how to overcome these handicaps, communicate with the world, and
spread her lectures promoting optimism. An inspiring read for everyone...   Biographies/Inspirational Pages 84*

☐

Sara Crewe *by Frances Burnett*   ISBN: *1-59462-360-0* **$9.45**
*In the first place, Miss Minchin lived in London. Her home was a large, dull, tall one, in a large, dull square, where all the houses were alike, and all the
sparrows were alike, and where all the door-knockers made the same heavy sound...   Childrens/Classic Pages 88*

☐

The Autobiography of Benjamin Franklin *by Benjamin Franklin*   ISBN: *1-59462-135-7* **$24.95**
*The Autobiography of Benjamin Franklin has probably been more extensively read than any other American historical work, and no other book of its kind
has had such ups and downs of fortune. Franklin lived for many years in England, where he was agent...   Biographies/History Pages 332*

☐

Name	
Email	
Telephone	
Address	
City, State ZIP	

☐ **Credit Card**   ☐ **Check / Money Order**

Credit Card Number	
Expiration Date	
Signature	

Please Mail to: Book Jungle
PO Box 2226
Champaign, IL 61825
or Fax to: *630-214-0564*

ORDERING INFORMATION

web: *www.bookjungle.com*
email: *sales@bookjungle.com*
fax: *630-214-0564*
mail: *Book Jungle PO Box 2226 Champaign, IL 61825*
or PayPal *to sales@bookjungle.com*

Please contact us for bulk discounts

DIRECT-ORDER TERMS

**20% Discount if You Order
Two or More Books**
Free Domestic Shipping!
Accepted: Master Card, Visa,
Discover, American Express

www.ingramcontent.com/pod-product-compliance
Lightning Source LLC
Chambersburg PA
CBHW080748250626
47162CB00010B/3060